A CROWN FOR Christmas

by

RACHEL VAN DYKEN

A Crown for Christmas
by Rachel Van Dyken

A CROWN FOR CHRISTMAS

Cover Art by Jena Brignola
Formatting by Jill Sava, Love Affair With Fiction

To Grandma Nadine,

I'm sad that you didn't get to read this before you passed, but know that you will always live on in every character I write. I'd like to think a part of you exists in every un-censored matriarch I come up with.

With all my heart, Rachel.

AUTHOR NOTE

Surprise!

It's no secret that I love Hallmark and am obsessed with every Christmas movie on the planet, I wrote this for fun but also because I was going through a hard time with my grandma passing and it seemed to be the only thing that put a smile back on my face when I needed it most. I think words have such a powerful way of helping us grieve, whether it be reading them or in my case, writing them. I hope you enjoy this fun little magical journey!

Thank you for being such wonderful readers to me, your support is everything. I'm genuinely so thankful for each and every one of you.

Happy escape and Merry Christmas!

PROLOGUE

Phillipa

THE FIRST TIME I met Fitz, or to most of the world, Duke Fitzgerald Geraldo Belleville, I punched him in the throat.

I was actually aiming for his chin. He was a few years older, clearly not wiser, but at least taller. So I missed my mark.

He started wheezing on his candy cane.

And well, the rest is history.

He died.

Long live the king?

Kidding, of course. He didn't die, but I did get grounded from the library for an entire month during the holidays, and the grand library is where they held the biggest ball of the year.

My parents, the king and queen, were huge into the holidays. We had people from all over the world visiting our castle for the ice sculptures alone, but the Holiday Ball? Well, it was the stuff of fairy tales.

And being a princess, it was one of the only times my mother ever let me wear my crown, a real diamond-encrusted tiara passed down to me through my great grandmother.

At twelve, I was finally going to be able to wear my hair in an updo with pieces of the crown poking out for all to see… and envy.

But instead of my grand entrance to the Holiday Ball, because of Candy Cane Choker, I was brought dinner in my room and sent to bed. Like a child.

My parents wanted to teach me manners, they said.

How to control the notorious Answorth temper.

Discipline and respect went hand in hand, they added as they kissed me goodnight and made me promise to stay in my room.

I didn't, of course, because along with the Answorth temper, I also inherited stubbornness. I supposed that would help me later on, if I ever had to look at that stupid Fitz ever again!

I fisted my hands and quietly made my way down the marble stairway. The Christmas music and laughter got louder the closer I got. The smell of pine trees and coffee, hot chocolate, pumpkin pie! My mouth was salivating by the time I made it to the bottom of the stairs and peeked around the corner.

"Shouldn't you be in bed?" Fitz grinned his stupid boy grin and shoved a forkful of pie into his mouth. Even the way he held the delicate gold plate made me want to launch myself onto his person.

He was rude.

Arrogant.

And he smiled at me like he was making fun of me.

And I hated being part of a joke I didn't understand.

He was fifteen.

I was twelve.

And still, he smiled at me like he knew a secret, and I glared back like I knew how to shove that fork right where the sun didn't shine.

"I can do what I want." I crossed my arms. "Shouldn't you be pulling candy cane shards from your throat?" I executed a fake coughing motion and wrapped my hands around my throat, making a face that hopefully looked like a frog that was dying a painfully slow death.

His demeanor darkened. "You could have killed me."

I shrugged.

"You're such a spoiled little princess." He sneered. "God, I hope I do not have to be your friend when you get old enough to know how to—"

"How to what?" I glanced over at him in curiosity.

"Be normal." He rolled his eyes. "I'm going to the party. You should go back to bed in the nursery. After all, that's what spoiled little princesses do. They sleep while the adults play."

I felt my lower lip tremble when the doors opened to the library and he was let in. I saw a flash of color, heard the music, and wanted so desperately to walk in there with my crown.

"Phillipa," Fitz called over his shoulder. "Don't kid yourself. You'll never be anything more than a girl trying to grow up too fast in a world where you won't ever belong."

"Why would you say that?" I whispered.

"Because. You're a stupid girl." He sneered as the doors banged shut behind him.

"I hate you, I hate you, I hate you," I chanted with each step I took back up the stairs to my bedroom.

I chanted it again as I lay down on my bed, arms crossed. I would never be his friend.

For all I cared, Fitz could just roll over and die!

CHAPTER ONE

Fitz

15 Years Later

"She almost killed me!" I pointed out, much to my mother's irritation. Already her left eye was twitching, and she was gripping the handle of her Hermès bag hard enough to leave nail prints on the soft cream leather. "Several times!"

She glared.

"On purpose," I grumbled. "Because she's a sociopath."

It was like every argument I had fell on deaf ears as the Bentley rounded the corner to the royal castle.

Answorth Castle to be exact.

One of the oldest, albeit smallest, royal families still in control of the country despite having a prime minister. With a country of only three hundred thousand people, it was nearly impossible to do anything without everyone knowing—

including the world.

And Phillipa… well, Phillipa held the proverbial keys to the kingdom.

God save us all.

Not only was she infamous for broken engagements, but her temper was the stuff of legends, exactly what I tried to point out to my mother—the woman who birthed me, brought me into this tedious royal world!

And still, she clutched her purse, looked straight ahead, and didn't even blink.

Hell, I'd be shocked if she was even breathing at this point. It didn't help that I had something in my pocket that was burning a hole through my trousers into my skin, making me feel like jumping into oncoming traffic—if there were any.

"It wasn't that bad," my mother finally said. "And you owe us this. You owe your country this."

"Ah, there it is." I leaned back in the seat, adjusting my tie for the fourth time as it noosed itself tighter around my neck. "I already told you it wasn't my fault."

"Fitzgerald." Shit, she just had to use my full first name, didn't she? "Your father and I—God rest his soul…" She made a motion across her chest. "…did everything we could to bring you up right. Being born of privilege seemed to only make it harder for you to understand why we had so many rules, why we still live by so many rules. You had one job."

"I did my job," I muttered, suddenly feeling ten again as she continued to threaten me over the single mistake I'd ever made in the public eye. Then again, it wasn't a small misstep. Nor was it something we could just dust under the rug, because when a man like me messes up, we go for the gold. Why settle for anything less, am I right?

"You got the prime minister publicly intoxicated doing Jell-O shots off a woman's… a woman's… a woman's…"

"Chest?" I offered, going for the tamer version of what had actually taken place. What the hell did she want me to do? We were in politics, he was having a rough day, I needed his support. So I got him blindingly drunk.

It should have worked.

The bar was completely closed off to the public.

Save one… person.

Phillipa.

Oh, I hadn't seen her there. I just had a hunch like I did whenever anything went wrong in my life. All signs pointed toward the spoiled princess with her too-tight dresses and god-awful crown.

Our soon-to-be queen.

It was the only thing that kept me up at night.

And the only thing that sent me to church still drunk last Sunday—I fervently prayed her mother would stay alive long enough to set someone else on the throne.

Anyone else.

Literally. Anyone. Else.

Mother let out another disappointed sigh. "You're nearly thirty, and now your face is all over the news as our country's newest bad boy duke."

I grinned and then hid it behind my hand with a cough when Mother shot me a glare that would make a lesser man weep—and often had on multiple occasions.

Intimidation was her hobby.

"Admit it, it's kind of funny."

"This is me laughing." Damn, crickets were making an appearance again in my head, weren't they? "It's the holidays.

Play nice with the queen, try not to get one of her maids pregnant, and for the love of God, don't get the PM drunk again or it's going to be impossible to marry you off."

"I already have a title. Why does it matter?"

Wrong thing to say.

She paled.

Her eyes bugged out of her face, and she raised that dangerously heavy purse above her head like a weapon.

Well. Shit.

Slowly she lowered the bag and inhaled, exhaled, probably prayed for patience, and then stared me down. "You're the only son, and while it seems archaic, you need an heir, and you need to marry royal blood. At this point, I don't care what country she comes from as long as she'll take you on and allow you to do the job that every generation before you has managed to do—blind, might I add!"

"Father wasn't blind; he had glasses. Big difference," I felt the need to point out, just in case she had forgotten.

"Let me speak!" She pinched the bridge of her nose as the car finally pulled to a stop. "Just… don't be the worst part of yourself that she manages to bring out. Be charming, smile, apologize for the bad press, and let's try to make it through the holidays without choking on any candy canes, hmm?"

"One time," I growled as embarrassment and anger boiled beneath my skin. She was insane. "And she sucker punched me, hardly ladylike."

"You made fun of her braids."

"I made an oinking noise and pulled. That's what boys do when they like girls. They make complete asses out of themselves and everyone around them because they lack the social skills to do anything more. The brain power alone it took to even touch her hair… well, let's just say I couldn't do math for at least a week."

"Ha ha." Mother rolled her eyes as the door opened and a white-gloved hand was held out.

She took it, head held high, and moved to the side as I followed.

"The Crown Princess of Answorth—" I drowned out the rest of it, my eyes greedily searching for her, my body preparing for battle, my mind ready to win the war of the wiles against her.

My archnemesis.

Rival.

The woman of my nightmares.

The hair on my arms stood up as if my body was preparing for the worst.

And then she appeared, much like a ghost during Christmas. You know, the ones with chains that tell you you're going to die? Like that. Only worse. Because she just had to be beautiful, didn't she?

Wavy, long black hair hung past generous breasts that were sadly contained by a tight, elegant, white leather dress and faux fur coat.

Red gloves.

Because she was clearly channeling Cruella De Vil and tortured puppies in her spare time.

And naturally, no boots, but red sleek high heels that looked ridiculous next to all the thick snow.

"And the Royal Crown Duke Fitzgerald Geraldo Belleville!" The announcement was made with fanfare as I stood before the woman who would soon be my queen and more.

And because my hobby was pissing her off, I bowed lower

than necessary, pulled a candy cane out of my pocket with a flourish, and handed it to her without grabbing her hand first. And then I brushed an open-mouthed kiss to her neck, inhaling deeply. She smelled like peaches and sin. Clever little witch just had to smell good, didn't she? "Nice to see you, Princess. Have you gained weight? Should I take the candy cane back?"

She was all smiles as she stilled and then pulled me in for a hug that had people whispering and coughing, and she murmured low in her throat, "Only if you're afraid it's going to get stabbed in your favorite appendage, which it very well might. Then again, I've always had horrible aim with small targets."

My glare should have set her on fire. "Touché."

"Nice to see you again. We roasted chestnuts."

"I'm allergic."

"I'm aware." Her grin spread wide.

"Well, at least this time you may actually follow through with it." I took her arm the way I was supposed to as we walked back up the stairs, my mother planning world domination behind us.

"What's that, Fitz?" Phillipa leaned in. I refused to smell the peppermint on her breath or feel the warmth of her skin—she was, after all, the devil, not like she'd be cold.

"My murder."

"It's been a lifetime of planning." Her grin was pure evil. I had half a mind to kiss it off her face just to even the playing field, shock the hell out of her, and get to taste the peppermint all in one fell swoop. Pity her lips were probably poison.

"How sweet." I winked. "To know you've been giving me so much thought."

Her smile fell.

We reached the top of the stairs, and I begrudgingly leaned over and kissed the back of her hand. I pressed my tongue against her skin mainly to throw her off balance, though it ended up making me nearly groan in pleasure.

Damn it!

Her skin was always so soft.

Her cheeks pinked when I pulled back and nodded. "Until later."

"Hmmm…" was all she said.

And I found that I liked the fact that she had nothing to say. And even more? The pink that still stained her cheeks as I left her alone in the entryway.

CHAPTER TWO

Phillipa

I LOATHED HIM.

And it was absolutely more loathing than what seemed natural to have toward another living breathing human being.

I hated the way he stared at me too long.

The way his perfect emerald eyes lingered like he was mentally mocking me and doing a bang up job of it.

But most of all, I hated that he was beautiful.

Hateful men shouldn't be beautiful. They should have warts on their faces, perpetual halitosis, and two lazy eyes.

He had none of those things.

In fact, the older he got, the more he aged backwards.

It wasn't even human!

He lacked even one gray hair—I tried finding one at the Christmas banquet last year after having a bit too much champagne and, through a mishap, plucked one that looked gray only to be ragingly disappointed when it was just a trick of the light.

He wasn't amused by my scientific research.

Then again, I wasn't amused with him. Ever.

I wasn't even sure why he was at the castle. It was my favorite time of year, and he was ruining everything with his swagger and arrogant smile.

I scowled after him and crossed my arms just as my mother rounded the corner and gave me a bright smile. "So, he's here?"

"*He*… can drop dead." I grinned and did a perfect curtsy then kissed each of her cheeks. The sweet smell of her Oscar de la Renta perfume floated into the air, reminding me to stay calm, to breathe, focus, and remember who wore the crown at the end of the day. My father, and next in line: me. "Now, why did you want to see me, and why is Satan visiting during the day? You know how he worships darkness."

Mother's eyebrows shot up. Her lips pressed into a thin line and then transformed into a perfect queenly smile as the Duchess of Belleville made her way into the entrance hall.

"Your Majesty." The duchess and my mother had been friends since they were children. I often wondered if it plagued them that Fitz and I didn't have the same easy friendship.

Then again, at least we had something, even if it was a feud that went back as far as I could remember.

"Nora." Mother waved her hand. "No formalities." They linked arms. "How was the drive in? Was there lots of snow?"

Nora grinned at Mother like they shared a secret. "Not too much, but I've heard rumors of a blizzard. Heaven forbid we get trapped here."

They both fell into ladylike laughter while I felt like my adrenaline had been trapped inside my body.

Trapped.

Here?

No.

Absolutely not.

Never.

No.

Hysterical laughter bubbled out before I could stop it. I covered my mouth with my hands and cleared my throat. "Sorry, just thought of something… funny." Like Fitz getting set on fire.

Nora smiled at me like she knew something I didn't.

My mother joined.

"Why am I suddenly terrified of what you're going to say next?" My body seemed to go numb. "Mother? Duchess?"

"Well." Mother ignored me, giving me her back while they started walking in the opposite direction. "I think some tea is in order."

A smile slid across my face, hopefully a pleasant one. Maybe I would get lucky and his would have arsenic in it.

I obediently followed after them, at least fifteen feet behind, while they talked in hushed tones.

The hallway was long.

I used to call it the hallway of the dead, thanks to all of my ancestors' paintings bearing down on me as a little girl.

Now that I'd just turned twenty-seven, I'd come to realize that I will join this hall one day, forever imprisoned in these walls. My memory would go on forever right along with them.

It was both jarring and exhilarating.

If only I could do it by myself.

But no, we just had to have an archaic rule that I needed to marry before I was able to receive the title of queen.

Goose bumps rose up and down my arms at the thought.

"Miss me, buttercup?" Fitz's voice jolted me out of my stupor. I scowled in his direction and kept walking to the double oak doors leading to one of my mother's favorite sitting rooms. It faced the north end of the estate and looked out over several water fountains and a rose garden that reminded me of a fairy tale on good days, and on bad days, made me wish those fairy tales still existed.

I could feel him next to me, feel the heat rising from beneath his impeccable three-piece designer suit.

His hand moved to the small of my back as he showed me into the room first. Technically, I did outrank him, but only because of the future title I'd receive.

He was still a royal duke.

Just as royal as me.

Unfortunately.

At least I'd be able to lord over him the rest of his miserable life once I was queen. That actually brought a smile to my face.

"Ah, you're so lovely when you smile," Mother commented as Douglas, one of her personal staff, pulled out her chair and then began pouring the tea with perfect precision.

He had the mind of an elephant, remembering everyone's preference: one sugar, extra cream for Mother, the same for the duchess, just cream for me, and all black for Fitz.

Complete shock.

He liked his tea black.

Like his soul.

I lifted the china to my lips and took a soothing sip, posture perfect, eyes on my mother as she smiled over at the duchess and set her tea down. "Well, shall we tell them?"

Next to me, Fitz stiffened.

He was rarely uncomfortable. I'd seen the man calm down the prime minister multiple times during a speech.

So why did his face turn a few shades whiter at the sound of my mother's voice?

And why did the duchess look so pleased? One would almost think she was about to marry into the royal family…

I gulped.

No.

No.

No.

Mother's grin widened. "We have an announcement to make. Well, actually, we're announcing it to you in preparation for the announcement you two will be making."

On the outside, I was the perfect face of calm and class. On the inside, I was using every swear word in the book and praying for the apocalypse.

"Your father and I have been concerned, you see, and now that he's passed." Mother gave me a sad look and then threw up her hands. "Every single person of interest has run away screaming."

Fitz laughed and then covered it up with a cough. "Sorry, tickle in my throat. Carry on… You were saying something about running away? Screaming? That sort of thing, correct?"

Had I been lesser born, I would have thrown my searing tea in his face and lunged for his throat. Instead, I took a sip. "It hasn't been that bad; it's not like any of them were you."

Mother gave me a funny look while the duchess had the good sense to stare at her lap. "Yes, it truly has. You refuse every single suitor."

"You do realize it's 2018, right? Women have the right to vote," I said through clenched teeth. "Do we really need to call them suitors like we're in our own version of *Aladdin*?"

"Does that make you Princess Jasmine?" Fitz just had to ask.

"I don't know," I replied tartly. "Does that make you the dumb tiger?"

"Rajah's my favorite character. Plus, better the tiger than the boy pretending to be a prince. What you see is what you get, sweetheart." He winked.

Yeah, knew that. Everyone in the kingdom knew that.

Thanks to the nude photos that surfaced from his trip to the south of France last year.

The newspaper was kind enough to censor out his lower extremities, much to the disappointment of every female on social media. All save one.

I took a solidifying breath. "I'll be fine. The law will pass, allowing me to rule without a man breathing down my neck, and all will be well."

"I'm afraid not," the duchess said with a slight wince. "You see, the prime minister is—how do I say this delicately?—facing some allegations of his own during this trying time. He needs to be focusing on the country, not your pride."

I tried not to flinch. "So I don't get to marry for love?"

"No," both women said in unison.

Mother added, "People like you don't get that luxury."

Her words wrapped around my heart, squeezing it so tight that only a few beats escaped before pain lanced through my chest.

The one thing I'd always asked my father.

The one thing I dreamed about when I was little.

Dancing with my fiancé at the Christmas ball.

And knowing that we would have more Christmases just

like that, looking into each other's eyes the way my parents did, as if the rest of the world should be envious of what they shared.

I tried more tea.

It suddenly tasted bitter on my tongue, so I set the cup and saucer down on the tray. "Am I to assume that's why you're both here?" I addressed the duchess.

She nodded to Fitz, who chose that perfectly nonromantic moment to drop to one knee and hold out a six-karat engagement ring with enough diamonds to blind a girl.

I stared at it.

Then I slowly raised my eyes to meet his. "You don't want this."

"I don't want this," he repeated. "But this goes beyond you, beyond me. This is what's best for the country. You—" He cleared his throat. "God, I'm going to regret telling you this, but you... you are what's best for our country right now. They need a distraction from politics. I'll be the first to admit that your shining personality makes me want to strangle you half the time, but I know what you do behind closed doors: the scholarships for the university, the anonymous investing in the food bank, the coat drives, the new hospital wing—"

I choked on my next breath, grateful I'd set my tea aside. "H-how do you know that?"

He grinned. "I have my ways."

Hot tears filled my eyes. This wasn't how I'd always planned it.

Not even close.

I had imagined snow.

The perfect kiss.

Happy, warm fuzzy feelings.

A little romance.

"Is that the best you can do?" I finally squeaked out.

Fitz grinned his movie star grin that had half the world panting after him. "Sorry, I'm a little out of practice. Not every day you ask the woman who tried to kill you to share her life with you." He winked and then whispered, "Candy cane killer."

I burst out laughing, covered my mouth with my hands, and shared an amused look with him.

"Marry me, Princess… please."

It was the please.

The way he looked at me, not through me, that did it. It released my heart just enough for me to hold out my left hand and whisper, "Yes."

CHAPTER THREE

Fitz

THE WORST STORM in over forty years.

That's what the news said.

Not at all helpful.

The mothers were talking wedding planning.

My phone was telling me that there was no escape.

Phillipa was staring straight ahead like she'd just gotten a noose put around her tiny neck, and I had at least three beads of sweat making the ostentatious journey down my back.

"Well." I stood and offered Phillipa my hand. "We'll just leave you ladies to it. After all, we can't be sitting indoors when there's perfectly good snow falling outside."

"We can't?" Phillipa narrowed her eyes.

I widened mine as if to say, *this is the only escape I'm offering you, take it or leave it.*

"I do love mint green." My mother clapped her hands

softly.

"But the royal colors are midnight blue and silver!" the queen scoffed.

I mentally communicated a neon sign that said *RUN* in Phillipa's direction. Thankfully, she stood and gripped my hand like a vise. "Yes, come along, Rajah. It's feeding time."

I threw my head back and laughed as we made our escape through the double doors and down the hall. "Do you know that completely takes the guesswork out of Halloween next fall? Much appreciated."

"Because last year's fox costume was such a stretch that, I imagine, had you any brain cells to begin with, they would have fried themselves on the spot and simply given up life altogether."

I gawked. "I'll have you know I sewed my own tail. Now, what do you say?"

"I say a man who gets a lot of tail should very well know how to sew one." She shrugged like it wasn't a complete dig at my past conquests throughout the years as one of the royal playboys.

Whatever, I was going with it, mainly because it made her cheeks red and her breathing short. And I loved the way the fire lit up her eyes when she felt like she was forcing me to be the proper royal. "I only wish they gave us a medal after so many one night stands, but alas, I'm prone to counting nothing but my participation trophies."

She stopped and glared. "Participation trophies? Like notches in your stupid bedpost?"

"No." I leaned in and tucked her hair behind her ear and whispered, "More like hickeys given and screams including my name over and over again, double points for an, 'Oh yes, right there, Fitz, right bloody—'"

She clapped her hand over my mouth. "You disgust me."

Her eyes said anything but.

How had I missed that?

The linger on my mouth that said she was curious.

Had that always existed?

Had I always wanted to explore the viper's nest just to see if I was immune to the bites?

"Yes, well..." I cleared my throat and sobered. "We can't all be perfect."

"I'm far from it," she admitted almost sadly. "Maybe that's the problem. I'm marrying someone I don't love—no offense—"

I waved her off. "None taken; do continue."

"I haven't had the opportunity to do anything outside this damn castle. I had guards at university just in case someone decided to kill me—"

"Which really isn't too far-fetched, if you ask me," I added and then grinned. "No offense."

She smirked. "None taken." Her steps slowed, and then she stopped and looked out the window. "Maybe I'm more like Princess Jasmine than I'd care to admit, scaring away every man who gets near... trapped."

I didn't realize my heart would care that she was sad, but before I could tell myself to run in the opposite direction, I was pulling her into my arms for a hug and kissing the top of her head. She smelled like fresh oranges and vanilla spice. I inhaled deeply and said, "I think everyone deserves an adventure."

"You would say that. You got the prime minister so drunk he ran around naked."

"Why does everyone keep fixating on the bloody prime

minister? He's his own man. So what if I handed him shots? He took them."

"Ah, lovely excuse." She tried to pull away. I held her firm.

I liked the way she felt in my arms.

I liked the way we felt together.

The blizzard was clearly the cause of some sort of alternate universe where she wasn't chasing me with a machete and I wasn't dreaming of using her as target practice.

"It's snowing."

"Your attention to detail is staggering. Tell me more," she said against my chest.

I couldn't help myself. I let out a little chuckle. "Well, let's go play in the snow."

"Play," she deadpanned. "Outside?"

We broke apart. "Why not? Is the princess afraid of a little cold?"

She crossed her arms. "No, it's just silly. Why would we prance around outside when we could—"

I silenced her with my finger. "Because if anyone deserves to let her hair down, it's you. Now, meet me in the main entry hall in thirty minutes. Dress warm."

She narrowed her eyes at me. "You're serious?"

"I'm always serious."

"Doubtful."

"Maybe you just don't pay close enough attention," I whispered soberly, grabbing her hand and pressing a soft kiss to her knuckles. "Thirty minutes."

"Th-thirty minutes." She stared down at her hand then back up at me. "I'll be ready."

"You'd think you'd be more excited about chucking objects that turn into ice at my face." I laughed at her suddenly excited expression. "Ah, there she is. Lovely. Well, try to at least keep the right side without ice scars, okay? It's my best side."

"No, it's not," she interrupted with a laugh and then shrugged. "Your left. You have a dimple at the corner of your mouth. Your left is your best side. Your right is your royal side, the one that doesn't show excitement at things like snowball fights."

I froze in place as a sense of intrigue stole over me. "Well, well, well, look who's been pining."

Vexation flashed in her eyes. "I would flip you off if I wouldn't get tattled on."

I crooked my finger at her. "And I would enjoy it more than you know."

CHAPTER FOUR

Phillipa

RIDICULOUS.

Fitz actually meant exactly what he said.

I had more important things to do, which was exactly what I told him over and over again until my voice grew hoarse, and I realized all words directed at him were falling on deaf ears.

Selective hearing.

"Come on!" Fitz started rolling a snowball between his gloved hands and winked. "You know you want to throw this at my face."

"I want to throw a lot of things at your face," I said through clenched teeth. "Sharp things, heavy things, fire-breathing things—"

He flinched. "I think I get the point." He held up his hand and then tossed me the snowball.

I caught it easily with both hands and stared down at it,

stark white against my black leather gloves.

Memories flooded.

Memories of a simpler time.

Of being a little girl running around the castle, playing in the snow, and getting in trouble for hiding from my tutor.

Hours spent in the forest close by, climbing trees and dreaming of true love's kiss and the day that the man I was supposed to be with would show up on a white horse and declare his undying love for me.

My parents should have locked up all the Disney movies.

Instead, they let my imagination run wild.

And when my father died, part of my heart died with him.

The part that was so intricately connected with him in a way that was impossible to explain.

He wasn't just Father.

He was Daddy in private.

He read me story after story about princes and said one day I would have one. One day I would rule the country. One day that prince would look at me the way that I deserved.

He told me to wait.

And now… now I had no choice.

The snowball began to melt despite the gloves on my hands.

"Princess?" Fitz was suddenly in front of me.

One sneaky tear slid down my cheek, most likely ruining my perfect makeup.

Fitz reached out and caught the tear, wiping it from my face. "If the idea of harming me brings you to tears, then I've been reading you wrong for a very long time."

All on their own, my lips formed a smile.

"There it is." He tilted my chin toward him. "I don't like it when you're sad."

"And here I thought it would cause you to burst into song and dance."

"Tears, regardless of where they originate, are never cause for celebration." He angled his head. "Care to share what weighs so heavily on your heart? Or would you rather inflict violence on my person?" His lips twisted into a wry smile. "I'm sure I could find a candy cane around here if you want a blast from the past."

I laughed and then tossed the snowball up in my hand. "I think I want to throw this between your legs and laugh gleefully when it misses its tiny target."

He burst out laughing. "Yeah, that's my cue to run."

"One," I warned with a grin. "Two!"

"Stop counting down!" He zigzagged around one of the trees lining the property. "Countdowns are never a good thing unless it's for New Year's!" He slipped a bit in the snow and then managed to trip over a bench that blended in with the white powder.

I ran after him.

Only to find a waiting victim.

One hand covered his face, the other between his legs.

"There's a bench…" I towered over him. "Right there."

"Caught that," he said, his voice a little tight. "But only after it bruised both shins and my pride." He blew out a sharp breath and then winked. "You gonna throw that?"

"Nah." I wasn't sure what possessed me to get down on his level, to drop the snowball and grab fresh snow and sprinkle it across his neck.

He moved to grab me.

I tried to get away.

He had me by the hips and tossed me onto my back then straddled me. "That went inside my coat. Snow isn't supposed to go inside the coat, Princess."

"It slipped." I laughed as he shook out his coat, dropping pieces of snow and ice on top of me. "And you're ruining my hair."

"I like you ruined." He leaned down. "You can admit it, you know."

"What?" I licked my dry lips as his head lowered until we were inches apart. My heart started to race. I had such a strong dislike for the man, and yet, my body had other ideas as his heat seemed to seep past my clothes and into my skin.

The smell of pine and cinnamon clouded all good sense.

And his ridiculously handsome smile had no right to be so… suggestive.

"You're having fun." And then he added, "With enemy number one."

"Has a ring to it, doesn't it?" I chewed my lower lip. "Now, get off me before I knee you in the balls."

"Touching them, even in a violent way, only encourages me to push you more. You know that, right?"

"What?" I whipped my head around. "Why would that encourage you?"

"Because…" He slowly got off me and then held out his hand. When I was standing again, he pulled me in and whispered across my neck. "You're more beautiful when you're fierce, and I couldn't stand being married to someone who refused to show every damn emotion on their face for the world to see."

"It's a fault," I said quickly, hating how close he was, how true his words were, and how they made me feel warm when it was freezing outside.

Fitz gripped me by the shoulders, his eyes fierce, gaze intense. "Never say that again."

"What?" I wasn't used to being bossed around. If anything, I bossed others around. It was part of the title. I suppressed a sigh. Already we were a disaster, weren't we?

"It's not a fault. Your humanity, your empathy, will always be your greatest gift."

Stunned, I stared at him. Really looked.

He was serious.

He was also right.

I opened my mouth to speak.

He pressed a gloved finger to it. "Don't ruin this moment by saying something hateful. It's a really good moment, here in the snow, talking like adults…"

I nodded.

He actually leaned in and kissed my right cheek and then drew a breath. I expected him to murmur something tender. Only, he whispered instead, "You've had mascara dripping down your right cheek for the last five minutes. A raccoon died in order to make that crap, didn't it?"

I smacked him.

He laughed and ran off.

And we were back at square one.

Lovely.

CHAPTER FIVE

Fitz

I FELT ITCHY.

Maybe it was the too-tight tux, or the fact that I had exactly ten days before Christmas Eve, before my marriage to a woman who would probably try to suffocate me with a pillow while I slept.

I didn't want to change my mind about her.

I didn't want to look at her and wonder if there was more beneath that icy exterior.

What I wanted was to do my duty and then live separate lives.

She wasn't supposed to smile at me.

Tease me.

Or bite that damn infuriating lip so much!

I clenched my fists and continued to walk decisively down the hall. I was staying in the room down the hall from her—a room that was more like a penthouse suite.

We'd recovered from our snowball fight.

Our claws were no longer sheathed, and the minute we both made it back to the main part of the castle, it was business as usual.

The light in her eyes was gone.

And I wanted nothing more than to shake her, or goad her… or kiss her… to get it back.

She needed more life, more… something.

And I needed to stop obsessing, or I was going to end up volunteering for the tedious job rather than enjoying the vacation at the castle with a decanter of whiskey.

I never took time off. I'd never had to. My only job was to make appearances and keep all of our political allies entertained.

There was no official name for what I did.

I'd like to think I was the one that always smoothed things over during stressful dinner parties.

I was a paid flirt at times.

And if necessary, a spy.

I was paid to attend events, paid to smile, paid to take pictures. The more I thought about it, the more annoyed I became when I realized that I'd always been the fixer for the crown.

Even when I was younger, I was fixing.

And I was doing it again. Only this time, I was the one getting sacrificed because of my titled blood and connections.

I gave myself another mental pep talk about duty and made my way into the dining room where wine was already being served.

I prayed to God for at least two bottles before the mothers

arrived.

The doors opened.

And there they were.

I almost hid under the table but grabbed the wine instead. "Your Majesty." I bowed low for the queen and then walked over to my mom, took her hand, and kissed it. "By your smiles, I imagine the wedding planning went well?"

"Perfect!" Mother beamed while the queen seemed to dance in place.

Were they that desperate?

"Good." I frowned a bit and took another sip of my wine. "And where would the lovely…" It nearly killed me to put an adjective before her name. "…Phillipa be?"

"Present." Was it my imagination or were her teeth clenched? She was wearing a gorgeous, red satin cocktail dress that left too many things to my imagination, like how did one put on such a thing?

Zipper?

Buttons?

I preferred zipper—faster that way. Buttons always took too bloody long. The sweetheart neckline gave me just enough view of her breasts to make my stare linger, and where it cut off near her knees, I saw nothing but perfect legs dipping into tall stiletto heels that looked more like a weapon than a shoe.

"Are you quite finished?" Phillipa asked.

I held up two fingers, then one, and nodded. "Now I'm finished."

With a scowl, she gave me her back. "Is this, or is this not, my wedding?"

"Our wedding," I interrupted. "Do continue."

I stared at her tense body as she faced both mothers.

"Yes, dear, of course." The queen tilted her head and frowned. "What's gotten into you? You look ready to cry."

"I can't." Phillipa took a deep breath. "I won't wear that dress."

My mother stiffened. "Now, Phillipa, that style of dress has been in our family tradition for generations. This is how things are done. You have the ceremonial ring from the duke, and you inherit the royal dress. You're more than welcome to make a few changes to the long sleeves, but it is tradition, I'm afraid."

"But—"

"Sweetheart." The queen shook her head slowly. "I'm afraid she's right; you must wear the dress. It's what the people expect you to do. You can't let them down."

"Fine."

I studied her, trying not to frown. She looked anything but fine. After a slight hesitation, I took it upon myself to grab a glass of wine and hand it to her.

She clutched it first then turned to look at me. "How'd you know to pick red?"

"The same way you probably know that that style of dress is horrible and should have been burned a few decades ago." The dress was the stuff of legends. Every queen wore the same court-style dress. It had enough panels, buttons, ribbons, and bows to make the wedding night seem like an Olympic sport of trying to find the person underneath all the clothing. It was customary to wear a veil that ran down the back of the dress hitting the ground. But it wasn't just that the dress was huge and extremely unflattering. It wasn't Phillipa's style, and for some reason, that bothered me.

Mother flushed, the queen looked ready to throw her drink

in my face, but Phillipa? Well, she looked ready to either kiss or strangle me—never could tell the difference with her.

She mouthed a *thank you* to me.

I winked. "But I guess traditions are traditions. Did you know, Phillipa, that we must release a Christmas goose along with seventy-seven doves the day we're married?"

My mother paled further while the queen frowned.

"Also, we have that old marriage bed… what is it called again? The Iron Reaper?"

Mother spit out her drink. I think she might have had a bit of a stroke with that one. "I believe we are supposed to…" I made air quotes. "…consummate our marriage while the church waits to examine the sheets—"

"You've made your point," Mother said in a stern voice. "It seems every royal marriage hasn't kept with all the… traditions." She turned to the queen, who was staring at me like she'd made a horrendous mistake in pairing Phillipa and me together.

Shocked, just shocked.

Did she know her daughter at all?

Furthermore, did she know me?

"Well…" The queen finally found her voice, did she? "If the duchess is amicable with the decision, I guess we could let Phillipa wear something else. It will be the first year it is done, so you may have some irritation and grumblings."

"Let me handle those." I lifted my glass. "Now, let's toast to a beautiful new tradition where the bride is free to pick out her own dress."

"Hear, hear!" Phillipa lifted her glass, took a sip, and then leaned over. I felt a squeeze on my hand and looked into her eyes as she whispered, "Thank you."

I felt those two words more than any other words I'd ever received in my entire life.

And I could have sworn, in that moment, my heart beat a little faster, as if it could find a way to chase after hers.

CHAPTER SIX

Phillipa

"You're following me," I quipped as my heels clicked against the marble stairs. All I wanted was a good book, comfortable clothes, and something to distract me from the fact that I had no control over my life and never would.

I'd always known it would be like this, that the crown would ask for everything, including my soul, and I would give it.

Wholeheartedly.

Because it was what my father had wanted.

I was an only daughter.

I was all they had.

And after a rough pregnancy, my father had decided that my mother wouldn't bear any more children. That was when it was written into our law that I could and would inherit the crown.

With my husband at my side.

Father had still been working on that part of the archaic law when he died of a heart attack, and Mother took it upon herself to continue his work.

But we learned very quickly that when it came to throwing our weight around, the least of our concerns was marriage laws.

When there was so much else to do.

"I'm not following, I'm spying." Fitz held out his hand. I took it as he helped me up the next few steps. "You look like you're in deep thought."

"Plotting." I grinned.

He stared at my mouth and then licked his lips like he wanted a taste, but that would be ridiculous. He hated me. I loathed him. It worked for us.

I shivered and looked away.

"I hate to interrupt what I'm sure are thousands of creative ways to decapitate me, but I thought we could go for a ride."

"A ride?" I crossed my arms. "In the car?"

"Er, no." He leaned in. "On a horse, about this high." He held out his hand. "Has fur and a braided tail, if I remember Mr. Wallaby correctly, and has a fascination with Golden Delicious apples and oats."

"Mr. Wallaby died." I cleared my throat.

His face paled. "Phillipa, I'm sorr—"

"Kidding." I winked. "But your face was worth it."

"Minx." He joined in my laughter. "Know that I was mere seconds away from buying you a horse."

"And how would you have managed that?"

"I would have snapped my fingers, of course, and told someone else to do it. I'm not an amateur."

"No." I sighed, swallowed by a wave of happiness. Wait,

why was I happy? What was going on? "You're not." I cleared my throat as he moved to stand in front of my door. "Is this going to be one of those times you force me to get out of the castle again?"

"Something like that." He tapped my nose with his finger. "Now, change into something warm—again—and meet me in the stables."

"I was going to watch a movie."

"A trade then," he whispered low, making my body sway when it needed to stay firmly in place, far away from his tempting mouth and those delicious stares. "You ride with me in the moonlight, and I'll bring you back not only safe and sound, but with promises to watch as much Hallmark Christmas Channel as you want."

I gasped.

"I know, I know." He put his hand on his heart. "Grand sacrifice on my part, but I know your obsession, Princess. It's beyond ridiculous, yet I can almost see your body twitching with need for its next fix."

I swatted him on the shoulder. "I'm not that bad."

"Two years ago, Christmas Eve Ball, you were late."

Warmth rushed to my face. "It was my dress."

"I call bullshit," he teased, his eyes sparkling with mirth. "Your dress was a simple, silver slinky thing that hugged every inch of your body. Your dress was magnificent. You had tears in your eyes, and I pestered you until you yelled at me and then confessed to wanting to finish the movie."

"How do you remember these things?" I wanted to stomp my foot in agitation, but I was afraid if I moved, I'd move toward him, and then I'd lean on him, and then I'd lift my head, I'd let him kiss me, and we'd be talking about a lot more than a ride and some Hallmark.

More like Netflix and chill, or whatever they called it.

"It's you." He shrugged. "How could I forget?"

"I can't tell if that's a compliment or an insult."

His full lips pressed into a wicked-looking smile. "A bit of both I'd think."

I shot him a narrow-eyed glare.

"Stop thinking so hard; you'll pull something." He put his hand on my shoulder. The heat radiating from his palm seeped into me and flowed all the way down to my toes.

What was happening to me? I couldn't possibly be attracted to him, could I?

I took in all the parts of him that I hated: his beautiful smile, his thick luscious hair, the build of his body, and then back to his smile, still trained on me. My heart sped up, beating a little on the ragged side, and my breath seemed to stall in my lungs. Fluttering began in my abdomen.

"Oh no."

"Oh no? What?" His perfect brows arched.

I shook my head. No, no, no, no!

"Um… I just…" My skin felt hot, needy, itchy. I waved him off in case he decided to step closer to me. "I'll just change real quick. Meet you in ten?"

"Phillipa? Are you all right?"

I opened the door to my room. "Yup, just forgot about an appointment tomorrow."

I inwardly cringed.

"Doctor?" he guessed while I tried to shut the door on his foot.

"No."

"Dentist?"

"Go away!" I shoved at his chest.

Why did he look so concerned?

"Are you feeling all right? Seeing a therapist already? Hmm?"

"Stop. Guessing."

"Marriage should be based on honesty," he said simply, like I should just confess all my darkest secrets to him in the hallway.

"Fine." Shoot, what was I going to say? "I um… have a bikini wax. Don't want to miss it because it… hurts," I choked out the word, "the longer you uh… wait."

Something flared in his eyes. "You know where to find me if you need company."

"Gross." I shoved him. "Even for you."

"I'll hold your hand!"

I slammed the door in his face.

"Moral support! That's what good soon-to-be husbands do!" he yelled through the door.

I burst out laughing. "You're so annoying!"

Silence and then, "Part of my charm."

"So you keep reminding me," I grumbled.

"Heard that."

"Go get changed!"

"Damn, that eager to go for a ride?"

I groaned into my hands. "You're impossible."

"I'll take that as a compliment!" he yelled again on the other side, followed by footsteps.

I exhaled in relief and went in search of some riding clothes that would keep me warm at night.

The temperature was below freezing at best, and I hated being cold. After grabbing a pair of thick winter leggings and a cable-knit sweater, I put on my fur boots, grabbed my fur earmuffs and matching scarf, and quickly made my way downstairs.

It wasn't until I was halfway to the stables that I realized.

I hadn't stopped smiling yet.

CHAPTER SEVEN

Fitz

A KNOCK SOUNDED at my door just as I was about to leave and head down to the stables. I had more nervous energy coursing through my veins than I knew what to do with, so I nearly bowled over the queen in my haste to see her daughter.

My fiancé.

Soon-to-be wife.

Nemesis.

Maybe I was coming down with something? It would explain the tightness in my chest every time I chatted with Phillipa, the shortness of breath, the dizziness when she smiled.

Son of a bitch, I would not fall for her.

I would not admit that I'd seen a crack in her cold exterior and that I'd fixated on that crack like a man on a mission to dig deeper and see beyond what she wanted the rest of the world to see.

Damn it, I was in deep, wasn't I?

The queen softly cleared her throat, pulling me out of my musings.

"Your Majesty." I bowed and opened the door wide.

"No." She held up her hand. Had she learned how to make every movement some kind of imperial gesture, or had it come naturally? "I'm not staying. However, I've been meaning to give this to you. I just wasn't sure…" She frowned as I stared down at the dark manila envelope in her hand. "I'm not exactly sure this is what he wanted when he died, when he gave this to me, but now that you'll be her husband, I do hope that you take the late king's words to heart."

"The late king?" I found myself repeating.

"Yes." She handed me the envelope. "They had a special relationship. She was never the same after he died. None of us were, but his passing altered her, took away some of the light that used to dance in her eyes. I'm sorry to say it was replaced with duty or death."

"Why is that?" I asked curiously.

She hesitated and then put her hand lightly on my wrist. "I believe we all handle grief differently, Your Grace. Phillipa decided she would be the best ruler our country had ever seen, next to her father. She poured herself into her duties. I'll never forget the day I saw her donating all of her old movies and toys, as if her childhood no longer meant anything." She swallowed. "She was nineteen. It was a hard year."

"Thank you." I gripped the envelope. Even through my gloves, it felt hot in my hand, as though it might flame to life any moment. Totally my imagination, of course. It was just an envelope, though it was quite weighty. I lifted it in her direction. "For this, I'll do my best."

She nodded and followed that with a smile that seemed to reflect relief. "Good. And Fitz? Please don't share this information with her, not yet."

It looked like she was about to say something else but changed her mind as she lifted her head, making me feel about two feet tall, and walked off, the hard click of her heels on the white marble floor the only evidence that she'd been there in the first place.

Chewing my lower lip, I stared down at the thick envelope and wondered what the late king could have possibly wanted Phillipa's future spouse to know.

With a grimace, I flipped the metal tab up and pulled out a heavy stack of documents.

On top of the stack was a cream-colored envelope that was waxed with the kingdom seal and addressed to *Future King.*

Me.

I would rule at her side as king, though my position would have less power than the queen.

I was about to help her run a kingdom.

Why hadn't I thought this through more?

Given myself time?

Oh, right. Mothers.

With a shaky breath, I opened the letter and nearly choked when I read the first few lines.

To Whom It May Concern:

You will never be good enough for my Phillipa. In fact, I loathe the idea that I even need to write a letter to a man who may one day take my throne and my daughter's love.

The idea is impossible to ponder.

It keeps me up at night.

The transfer of power, and the idea that she might find a love so powerful that even my own doesn't compare.

None of this, of course, matters, for you still won't ever be good enough to kiss her feet let alone hold her close.

But that is what a dying man asks of you.

My final wish is that she finds someone who tries every single day to be worthy of her laughter, worthy of her smiles, worthy of every single word that flows from her mouth, good or bad.

I need to know that, even in my death, she still has someone trying, with every breath of life they are given, to make her smile.

She doesn't like being bossed around. Do it anyway.

If she yells at you, it just means you've provoked her, but you've probably discovered that *early on in the relationship.*

I stopped reading and barked out a laugh. But the missive called to me, drew me back in, and once again, I began reading the strong, perfect handwriting.

She used to believe in fairy tales.

In knights riding in on horses. My fault, I suppose, and the fault of growing up as an actual princess likely causes you to believe that you do, in fact, get your happily ever after.

Alas, those aren't promised to us all.

And Disney rarely includes the work that goes behind running a kingdom.

Love her well. Love her right. Love her the way she deserves. And never forget that you are the lucky one. Not her.

Live by that code, and you should do just fine.

Betray me, and I'll dig up my own grave to haunt you as a ghost.

You think I'm joking.

I rarely joke.

I now bequeath to you, young man, my greatest

treasure.

Her heart.

These old hands can no longer keep it, and I cannot take it to my grave, though I mourn its loss even as I still hold it in my hands.

Be good.

Be fair.

Be humble.

Be hers.

Signed,

The Royal Majesty,

King Elliot Marcus Answorth

I don't know how long I stared at the familiar handwriting, but it was long enough to feel my eyes mist at a dying man's last wish.

Long enough to feel like I had a greater responsibility than I was ready for. And long enough to wonder what it would be like to have that sort of devotion from another human being.

Was it even possible?

The thought haunted me the entire walk to the stables.

His words had put me in a depressed mood. Who could possibly live up to those standards? Especially now that our marriage was completely arranged. Was that why the queen looked so upset?

I didn't have any time to think more about it, since the

minute I looked up, a snowball came sailing toward my face, hitting me square in the nose.

"Son of a bitch!" The words exploded out of me as I stumbled forward, gripping my nose. Hell, was it bleeding? "I think you killed me."

"I didn't throw it that hard," came her sweet, syrupy voice, and then warm, no longer gloved hands touched the sides of my face.

Stunned, I just sat on a nearby cement bench and let the feel of her hands register. Heat suffused my face and then fanned out all over my body. My heart decided to beat harder than it should, and I could have sworn more dizziness took over as I stared into her concerned gaze. "Are you okay?"

"No," I whispered hoarsely. "I may need you to kiss it and make it better."

She rolled her eyes and kissed the middle of my forehead. "Better?"

"You missed." I grinned and then pulled her in for a kiss.

Her subtle scent swished over me, teasing my senses. Her body seemed to melt against mine, and something stirred inside me—down to my soul.

Yup, definitely coming down with something.

Passion.

Lust.

Need.

She moaned into my mouth. I needed no encouragement to prolong the best kiss of my life. A kiss that would light a city on fire and keep its tenants warm for millennia.

Her lips were pillow soft; she tasted like the wine she'd been drinking and the peppermint candy I'd seen her swipe after dinner.

I licked the seam of her lips, earning a gasp. As I deepened the kiss, she dug her hands into my hair and pulled my face even closer. Then she loosened her grip and slid her arms around my neck. The rough knit of her sweater scratched across my exposed skin. It was one of the most intimate and exciting sensations I'd ever experienced.

I couldn't stop.

I needed to stay in that moment, with her in my arms, forever.

Just like that.

Where we weren't arguing.

Throwing hateful comments or, in her case, sharp objects.

A horse neighed; another answered.

We broke apart.

Both gasping for air.

Both staring at each other in fascination and wonder.

"Healed." I swiped my thumb across her wet lower lip.

"Miracle," she countered right away with a smirk, grabbing my hand and kissing my thumb.

Bloody hell, my body felt suddenly weak. Weak with need for her, for my enemy, for a woman who would thrill at seeing me run over by multiple cars.

And then I remembered her father's note.

"Shall we?" I offered my hand and cleared my throat.

She took it.

I felt the disappointment swirl in the tense air between us.

We'd found common ground all right.

Explosive lust and attraction.

Marriages had been built on less.

But after reading his words, I suddenly craved more, and like a lunatic, I picked and picked and picked at the words, their meaning, the tiniest nuances, and I became determined to discover everything I could in the next few days about the woman I would share my life with.

"A warning," she said once she was on her horse and smiling back at me.

"Oh?" I grinned.

"I like fast." She laughed and then she was off.

I let her go.

Enjoying the sound of her laughter.

And wondering, for once, if there wasn't more joy in losing when you have a worthy opponent.

CHAPTER EIGHT

Phillipa

WHAT HAD I been thinking?

I hadn't, really.

I'd just… reacted.

Out of curiosity.

Out of need.

I pushed my horse faster. "Come on, boy."

I could feel him even though I couldn't hear him. Fitz was gaining on us, and I wanted nothing more than to beat him then rub his face in it.

Then kiss again.

More than once.

Ugh, this is where a best friend would come into play. A best friend talked some sense into you, handed you wine, and told you to move on.

I had no close friends.

I refused to let anyone get too close for fear of what would happen when I inherited the crown. Would they change? Would I?

Maybe that's what Fitz meant about fun.

I was pushed into adulthood at fourteen when fathers heart originally started failing and had never looked back. And now that I was getting ready to take over the kingdom, I felt a sudden loss of all the things I never did and should have done, like race a wicked scoundrel through the trees just because I could.

I reached the heavy tree line and stopped my horse. He huffed out an irritated huff. Mr. Wallaby always did like to run fast. A gift from my father before he died, he was older, but you wouldn't know it.

"Breakneck speed." Fitz laughed when he stopped his mount, Demon, next to mine. I had told him I'd named the horse after him to be mean, when really it was his dark black hair and eerie white tail that had inspired me. "Who taught you to ride like that?"

My smile fell. "My father."

"I'm sure he'd be proud you kicked my ass." Fitz winked. "Probably cheering from heaven and trying to find some rock for me to trip on later just to rub it in."

I laughed. "He was always a gentleman. I don't think he would have deliberately tripped you, and if he did, it would be an accident."

"Right, just like he would accidentally clean his hunting rifles whenever I came over for the holidays."

I laughed harder. "It was for the Christmas hunt and you know it."

"Five days in advance? Every day? With no use in between?"

He narrowed his eyes suspiciously. "Pretty sure the only thing that kept him focusing on cleaning those guns was aiming them at my body with a smile on his face. Do you even realize how many times he pulled me aside and scolded me for just… existing?"

I rolled my eyes. "He would never."

We turned our horses and started trotting back toward the stables. "Oh, he did, when I'd just turned twenty-two. I came home from university and straight here for the holiday celebrations. He found me with… well, let's just say I was with a nice young lady. He caught me by the ear, dragged me out into the snow, and told me to dig."

I stopped my horse. "Dig what?"

"Snow." He shrugged, pulling his horse to a stop. "The lovely sidewalks were cleared for the rest of the guests by five a.m. When I was finished, he asked me if I'd learned my lesson."

"What did you say?" I was enraptured. How had I never known this?

"Yes!" He laughed. "I'm not insane! I said, 'Yes, Your Majesty,' and then, of course, he just had to ask me what the lesson was."

"Did you lie?"

He made a face. "One never lies to his king."

I didn't want my respect to soar.

But it did.

Just like my heart.

"So what did you say?"

"I said he should probably tell me before I had to dig a trail to China." His smile was infectious. "And so he led me to one of the blistering cold cement benches, where we sat, and he said, 'Kisses are like treasure. A wise man will invest, save. He'll be cautious whom he shares his treasure with. You see, the person must be worthy of the treasure, but you also don't want to be the sort of person to forget the value of it as well. When you share your kisses with a woman whose name you don't even know, you don't value the treasure you're sharing or what you've been given in the first place. The treasure, you see, loses its value, and so do you.'"

I sucked in a breath as tears filled my eyes.

He offered a sheepish smile. "So I vowed to him right then and there that I would guard my treasure."

"I like that story."

"I hated it at the time. Never fun to be discovered with your pants around your ankles and your naked ass pointing toward His Majesty, but there it is."

I burst out laughing. "So, how long did you last?"

He locked eyes with me and whispered, "Until about twenty minutes ago."

And then he was leading his horse ahead of mine back to the stables, and I sat there, slack-jawed, watching him go.

CHAPTER NINE

Fitz

WHAT THE HELL had possessed me to even tell her that? I had a certain reputation to uphold! Then again, there was a very good reason I was the fixer of the family: because I'd stopped being the one that messed everything up.

I didn't kiss women.

Not since that night.

I lusted.

I touched.

I flirted.

I was tempted.

But every single time I was faced with an opportunity to take someone back to my flat in town, or even one of our homes in the countryside, I couldn't do it. I saw his face—his eyes, his lips—every time.

And after reading that letter, I was once again brought

back to a time when I would never be good enough to even stand in the same room as the man.

And yet, he'd taken time to teach me an important lesson, one that I should have still remembered when I kissed her.

But the pull was impossible.

I justified it by telling myself we'd soon be married. It wouldn't be wise to just jump into bed together and yell surprise at Phillipa—that was an easy way to get a sword through the chest or a Taser to the lower extremities.

My body gave an involuntary shudder as I led the horse back into the stables and waited for Phillipa.

She got off her horse with ease, the only way a royal like her did anything. I looked away and handed the reins to one of the stable hands as she did the same.

We walked in silence.

Well, not really silence.

We walked in tense, snow-crunching silence.

A glistening layer of ice had frozen over the snow, making it loud as hell as we made our way back to the house.

"No one? Really?" she asked once the doors were opened for us and the heat from the castle billowed out into the snow.

"Really." I sighed and stared down at the wonder on her face. Her cheeks were flushed, her lips pink. Damn, those lips looked good enough to lick again; I should have taken my time. I stared harder than a man who wasn't in love should.

And I wondered in that moment if her father was somehow bossing people around in heaven.

How else was this possible?

This intense attraction I suddenly felt for her. This need to chase her, only to catch her again and kiss her.

When I thought of Phillipa on the way here, all I could

think about was violence and the prospect of finding myself thrust down the stairs.

But now?

Now.

"You shouldn't have wasted a good run on me," she said breathlessly.

"A good run?" I repeated in confusion.

"You know." She waved a gloved hand between us. "A good run being you were doing so well; you shouldn't have wasted that kiss on me."

Her words and body language didn't match.

My lips turned up into a slow smile. "Oh? So you take it back?"

"I didn't say that."

"You kind of did." God, I loved annoying her.

"Fitz." Her voice was not amused, and yet I saw it on her face, clear as day: she liked it as much as I did, the constant fighting, the wonder if you were seconds away from getting tripped, chipping your tooth on the marble floor—again.

"Phillipa," I rasped, reaching for her because I couldn't help myself, and was interrupted by a matronly throat clear.

"Ah, there you two are." Mother clasped her hands together. "Whatever were you doing outside? It's freezing!"

"I wasn't cold," Phillipa said under her breath, and I found myself wrapping a protective arm around her, even though Mother was harmless. I just… I wanted this moment for myself, for us. No intruders. God, look at me. Day one and I was already losing my bloody mind.

Mother's eyes narrowed in on both of us. She saw more than I'd like her to see—not that there was anything wrong with actually liking one's fiancé and not wanting to run her over with a horse.

The irritating fact was that if she did find out that I'd kissed her, she'd say something hateful and offensive like, "I told you so."

God save the queen.

I'd rather apologize to Phillipa for being an ass my entire life, while giving her unlimited access to candy canes, than hear those words from my mother's lips. Maybe that explained why I was itching to get as far away from her as possible. Maybe that's why I decided to stay good on my promise when I was suddenly exhausted and tempted—oh so tempted—to do more with Phillipa's mouth.

"Yes, well, we have a date… with the Hallmark channel." I grinned. "I lost the race, ergo, I'm about to be subject to an entertaining story about a widowed prince in some far-off country in need of a nanny, or maybe a tutor, or even better, he's in need of a wife, and wouldn't you know? One of his staff members locates the perfect candidate and whisks her away to this far-off country where everyone judges her American accent, her clothes, and don't even get me started on the ex-girlfriend who shows up to meddle, or the daughter, maybe even son, who despises everyone but suddenly falls in love with the nice young woman who was just trying to make it a good Christmas." I wiped away a fake tear. "Then again, we could watch the one about the Christmas festival—oh wait, that's probably at least half of them. Most of the time, they're about to be ruined, but wait! Your ex-boyfriend from high school, first love…" I winked at Phillipa's annoyed expression. "First kiss." I gave her a shocked look.

"First homicide?" she interjected.

I covered my chest with my hand. "I'm wounded."

She rolled her eyes. "I know they're all the same. I know the ex saves the day, they fall in love, and it's the best Christmas in decades, but I just… I love that you know it's all going to be okay." Her lower lip trembled.

I caught the movement.

My mother was too busy examining me as if I suffered a severe head wound and needed medical attention.

"Well." I pulled Phillipa close. "We should go. Did you need anything else, Mother?"

She narrowed her eyes. "No, I was just—well, it's about the ceremony on Christmas Eve, but it can wait."

"What about it?" Phillipa asked, adopting a suspicious tone.

"Well…" Mother looked uncomfortable. Holy God, we needed whiskey—fast. "Typically, your father would walk you down the aisle."

I felt Phillipa tense next to me.

"But the prime minister has already volunteered to do the honors. That is, if you agree."

I loved the guy.

But she was mine.

Mine to touch.

Mine to hold.

Mine to walk.

"No," I blurted.

Both Phillipa and Mother craned their necks at me like I'd just stripped naked and done a little pole dance to the *Magic Mike* soundtrack.

"What I mean…" I cleared my throat. "Is, er… No."

"Did he mean to repeat himself?" Phillipa asked Mother.

I sighed. "I was hoping…" Mentally, I was strangling myself

so I'd stop talking. Physically, my mouth just kept opening and dumping out words that formed illogical sentences. "That I could have the honor of walking Phillipa down. I think..." My throat closed up as I thought of the late king, of her relationship with him. "And if that seems too unconventional, the only other person I think worthy of walking Phillipa down would be the queen herself."

Gasping, Mother tensed. "It hasn't been done," she choked out. "Ever."

"Well..." I shrugged. "It doesn't mean it can't be done at all, does it?" I winked at her and then turned my attention to Phillipa.

Mother let out an exasperated sigh. "We'll discuss it later. Good evening."

I knew what that phrase meant; it meant I was going to have to fight her on it, but it was Phillipa's wedding. In a world where she couldn't control much, shouldn't she at least be given the opportunity to control this? I wondered if she read my thoughts as my mother walked off. When she finally made it around the corner, I exhaled and announced, "Let's grab some liquor before you subject me to Hallmark."

Phillipa let out a laugh that I felt in my bones, in my very soul.

Damn it, day one, man. Hold it together.

"We could always turn it into a drinking game."

"I think I just fell in love." I laughed as I picked her up and swung her around. "Should we take a shot each time someone wears red?"

She burst out laughing as I set her on her feet. "We'd be drunk at opening credits."

"How about..." I leaned in. "Each time a character laments

about a past love gone wrong?"

"Again, drunk, next!" She supplied another free laugh that had me ready to pick her up again, only this time I wanted to toss her over my shoulder, move in the opposite direction, and have her all to myself.

Actually...

"You have a flat screen in your room?" I asked casually.

"Everyone does." She shrugged.

"Lovely, I'll meet you there in fifteen. Get comfortable and prepare to have your life changed."

"Because of whiskey or Hallmark?" she challenged with a grin.

"A little bit of both." I leaned down and pressed a kiss to her cheek. "Present company included."

She sucked in a sharp breath. "You know, I can't tell if you want to kiss me again or if you're just baiting me so you can pull my hair and chase me down the hall."

My body tightened. "I don't think I've ever wanted to pull someone's hair more in my entire life, not in an effort to chase them, but to pull them so closely to my chest that all I feel is their skin, their breath, and maybe a soft moan of pleasure."

Her eyes flickered to my mouth, and her lips parted. "This is crazy."

"I'm going to just go with it and stop asking why I want nothing more than to kiss you senseless."

She wrapped her arms around my neck. "I still want to push you down the stairs."

"Yes, well, you wouldn't be you if you weren't planning every single way to cause physical harm to my person, now would you?"

"Not at all."

"And…" I cleared my throat. "I wouldn't be me if I didn't say exactly what was on my mind exactly the minute I had a thought." I brushed a light kiss across her lips. "I'm annoyed at how strikingly beautiful you are. Always."

"Funny, since my biggest complaint is that you're not ugly," she countered.

I barked out a laugh. "Sorry to disappoint."

"It's not fair."

"Life isn't fair, but at least you'll be saddled with a trophy husband, eh?"

"Saddled? No, I'll be joined with a partner in crime, who's tempted to both strangle and kiss me all at the same time."

"It's like I have an angel on one shoulder going, 'God she's beautiful, we should kiss,' and a devil on the other shoulder going, 'God she's beautiful, make sure you strike first.'"

Phillipa grinned. "You know, if we're planning on watching a movie…"

"Right." Had we seriously been just staring at each other in the hallway, laughing, flirting? I gave my head a shake. "Fifteen minutes."

"Yes." She gave me a shy smile as we both walked in silence to our rooms.

And when I closed my door and saw the stack of papers from her father, curiosity got the best of me. I read another, and another, and then another before finally getting dressed and having the staff bring over a decanter of whiskey to her room.

With each footstep, my smile grew.

"In order to win the treasure, you must first earn it. You aren't worthy—never will be—but the idea is that each and every day. You. Try."

His words of advice to her future husband.

To me.

And he'd said treasure.

Coincidence?

I wasn't sure, but I'd like to think he was cleaning his guns in heaven and staring down at me while God painted a giant target on my back that read, "Good luck."

CHAPTER TEN

Phillipa

I TOLD MYSELF it was crazy that we were actually getting along, that we had shared more than one kiss, and both of us still had all our limbs, and he wasn't suffering a head wound.

It was madness.

Right?

I tried not to overthink the fact that he would be in my bedroom alone with me, and if my mother found out, there would be hell to pay. After all, a princess always made sure she showed complete decorum in all she did.

Why was it that Fitz was making me want to push my own boundaries?

The doubtful realist side of myself said he was doing this on purpose to get me to misstep and cancel the wedding, or something equally horrible.

What if he was pushing me on purpose?

What if he had other intentions?

It would make sense, but why the cease fire now?

I quickly changed into a pair of leggings and a loose hoodie that my mother had threatened to burn if I ever wore it in public again.

As if Nike was beneath us or something.

I pulled my hair back into a braid just in time for a knock to sound at the door.

"Come in." I cleared my throat.

Melly, one of the kitchen staff, winked as she entered. She was around my age and had always been good to me, though she never crossed the boundary of staff member and royalty, much to my disappointment. My title did more than prevent me from fun; it also prevented me from tight friendships, she was the closest thing I had growing up.

My stomach sank a bit as I swallowed back the bitter sting of tears. "You can just leave the whiskey decanter and glasses on the table."

"Refreshments for two," she said with a sly smile. "I'm happy for you."

And she was; I could tell by her mischievous smile. "I trust this won't be… discussed?"

"You mean the fact that I just saw the duke make his way down the hall before I knocked, or the fact that he looked just as comfortable as you? Honestly, I think it's the matching smiles that give it away." She winked.

"The most you've ever spoken to me in one breath and you use it on the duke?" I crossed my arms and smiled, obviously teasing.

She just shrugged. "He likes you; he's always liked you. Unfortunate, it was, that I took the bet you'd get together right after you finished university—"

"What?" I whipped my head around. "What do you mean? The bet? What bet?"

She grinned. "The entire staff has been wagering for years down to the exact month and year when you two would fall for each other."

"This is an arrangement," I corrected.

"Uh-huh," she said sarcastically. "Absolutely, just an arrangement between two people who have absolutely no attraction whatsoever to one another."

I narrowed my eyes.

"It's okay, you know," she said in a soft voice. "At the risk of getting sacked, it's okay to like him, Your Highness."

I felt my lower lip tremble.

Two steps later, she opened her arms.

And I was hugging her desperate for someone to tell me everything was going to be okay."What if it's not real?"

She rubbed my back. "What if it is?"

I wiped under my eyes.

"Now." She stepped away, grabbed my hand, and squeezed. "Dry your eyes and try to have a good time. Besides, rumor has it he's been on your side every step of the way when it comes to the wedding. Not every man would do that, especially a royal."

I jumped when a loud knock sounded at the door. "That's him."

Melly gave me a funny look and then went and opened the door. "Good evening, Your Grace. I was just leaving."

Fitz's smile could have melted snow. "Hello, Melly, how's your father? I heard he had a bit of a fall on the ice last week."

Melly beamed. "He's recovering quite well. Thank you for the flowers."

Stunned, I watched the exchange in slack-jawed silence.

"Of course!" He smiled brighter as she left the room and shut the door quietly behind her. Fitz met my gaze. "What?"

"You… you…" I jabbed my finger in his direction. "You don't even live here!"

"First of all, our properties are next to one another. Second, as much as it pains you, this has always been like a second home to me—"

"Much to my frustration," I grumbled. "How did you even know?"

"Ah…" He tapped his temple with his finger. "I know all."

"Doubtful."

"Try me," he snapped in a confident tone.

"What did I get for my eighteenth birthday?"

"You mean other than breasts?" he clipped, his voice colored by humor.

I scowled and crossed my arms. "That's completely inappropriate!"

"And yet, one hundred percent true." He swaggered toward me—or at least that's what it felt like. "And what I think you're referring to is the Maserati SUV that your mother had waiting for you in front of the castle. Finally, your own vehicle because you were done allowing people to drive you everywhere—your words, not mine."

"But—"

"You were wearing a silky black tank top that was tucked into these cream pants that held my attention not because of their texture—though that looked nice too—but you looked so… grown up in that moment, so royal, that I felt…" He cleared his throat. "It doesn't matter how I felt."

"It does." I hung on every word. Please, God, don't let him

be playing me. "It matters."

He tilted his head at me and shoved his hands into the pockets of his joggers. For some reason, it looked natural, him wearing athletic gear; God knew he'd spent at least half his adult life in the gym. The guy had a six-pack on his six-pack—not that I knew or that I'd followed it as it was trending on Twitter last summer when he vacationed in Belize.

"Sad." He swallowed slowly. "I felt sad."

Not what I expected. "Why would you feel sad?"

"Because, you were all grown up without ever having the chance to be a kid. I was busy sneaking out of my bedroom window when I was eighteen, Meanwhile, you were getting taught how to help run a country while your fathers health continue to decline. We're both royal, but make no mistake, Phillipa, your childhood was cut short the minute your father got sick. So yes, I was sad. I'm still sad, because I wish I could give you those precious years back where the world wasn't looking to you—to us, one of the last remaining monarchies—to do things right." He exhaled as though realizing he'd said too much, and I felt the sting of tears again.

All my life, I'd thought I had nobody.

All my life, my only enemy had been my only friend.

I rushed toward him, and he looked panicked, like I was about to slap him. A moment later, he moaned when I pressed a hand on each side of his head and pulled him down for a kiss I felt everywhere a woman is supposed to feel a kiss. Heat descended between our two mouths; fire lit my body as I pressed myself against him.

He lifted me into his arms, deepening the kiss, massaging my tongue, making me ache for more as I clung to him for dear life.

"What was that for?" he whispered in between more kisses. Kisses that felt like promises of a future where I wouldn't be alone anymore, where I'd have someone to share the burden with.

I kissed him again and pulled back. "That was for seeing me. For always seeing me, even when you wanted to strangle me."

His lips lifted into a smile. "Yes, well, when feelings aren't reciprocated, a person does whatever they can to gain attention, even if it means stepping outside someone's favor."

"Is that your twisted way of saying you'd rather pull my hair and irritate me than ignore me?"

"Ah, Princess, when I pull your hair, it won't be irritating. I can promise you that." He winked.

Flames of embarrassment licked at my face.

"Now…" He slid his hands down my arms and then braced my hips. "Let's get this Hallmark business over with."

I gasped. "One does not get Hallmark 'over with'! It's an experience! A way of life!"

He bit down on his bottom lip. "You're cute when you're excited."

"Hallmark gets me excited."

"Want to know what gets me excited?" He eyed my mouth again.

I pressed a hand to my chest. Why was my heart beating so fast? "I'll just pour the whiskey."

"Ignore this all you want, Princess, but you're going to be mine soon, remember that."

Funny he should say that.

Since I already was… irrevocably… his.

CHAPTER ELEVEN

Fitz

SHE FELL ASLEEP in my arms.

Snoring.

I took one video and two pictures.

Blackmail for later; old habits die hard, and I'd like to think part of our special relationship included the competitiveness and teasing between us.

I didn't sleep a wink.

I did, however, spend a considerable amount of time staring at her in wonder.

She clung to me like she had nowhere else she'd rather be. We'd only made it through one of the movies before she closed her eyes.

I drank more whiskey.

And was damn near drowning in her scent and ready to throw myself out the highest window—I wanted her.

Desperately.

This was not how it was supposed to be.

She was supposed to be hateful.

Maybe I'd just made her my enemy for so long because she rejected me. Funny thing was, I didn't think she even remembered all the times she rejected my friendship. I was too afraid to put my heart out there, especially since my friendship had always been stomped all over.

So I teased her.

And I told myself that the stupid ache in my chest was a sickness.

The sickness was her.

"Mmmm…" She stretched and blinked up at me. "Is the movie over?"

"Not just the movie, but the day. Tell me, Princess, is this the first time you've had a man in your bed?"

She jolted and then grabbed a pillow. I ducked before it could connect with my face, only to get hit during her second try.

"That hurt!" I roared, jumping to my feet on her bed and grabbing the first pillow I could find.

"Be an adult!" She burst out laughing. "You're fine!"

"'Tis merely a flesh wound," I joked. "But now I have to turn the other cheek. After all, it's in the Bible."

She looked up like she was waiting for something.

"What?"

"Nothing." She shrugged. "I just expected more lightning bolts, at least some warning thunder."

"Hilarious."

"It's not every day the devil quotes scripture." She winked.

"Wasn't quoting, not the devil." I lifted the pillow high.

"Now, stand still."

She jumped off the bed. "Says the guy that's gonna toss a pillow at me."

"I was thinking less toss, more smacking, striking? Damn, I'm trying to find the right word."

"Phillipa?" the queen's voice sounded on the other side of the door. "Are you decent? We need to chat."

I froze.

She knocked.

My panicked expression must have said it all as Phillipa grabbed my hand and then shoved me toward the adjoining walk-in closet.

"No, wait—" I braced my hands against the door. "At least let me hide in the bathroom!"

"And if she has to use it?" Phillipa argued.

"Valid," I grumbled and let her close the door behind me.

"Phillipa?" The queen sounded frustrated. "Why aren't you dressed? And were you talking to someone?"

"TV. You know me and the Hallmark channel." The woman couldn't lie to save her life. I rolled my eyes and waited to be discovered, only to have the queen let out a disappointed sigh.

"Honestly, Phillipa, you have better things to do with your time."

"I was spending it with my future husband," Phillipa argued. "And since we're going to be married in less than ten days, I figured it would be a smart move."

Well done!

"About that…" Her mother sounded funny. Why did she sound funny? "I have news."

"Oh?"

"You should sit."

My palms started to sweat.

"It seems that the Royal Duke of Germaine has changed his mind. You see, after his mother's recent death, he's re-thinking his responsibilities to his family and—"

"He needs money," Phillipa said in a sad voice.

"Don't be crass," the queen scolded. "And he has one of the oldest titles next to Fitz. I just wanted you to know that you have options." Silence fell. Then, "Why aren't you jumping up and down?"

"Options." Phillipa sounded like she was weighing the word.

My life flashed before my eyes.

A life without her.

A life without children.

Holy God, where did that even come from?

A pang hit my chest, swiftly, effectively, causing momentary insanity as I jerked open the closet door and announced, "I object!"

Phillipa's face paled while the queen looked so scandalized that you'd think I'd just appeared naked. I had all my clothes on.

"Fitz," Phillipa said with clenched teeth. "What a surprise."

"Oh, please, you couldn't lie to save your life and mine." I rolled my eyes. "You know I've been here since last night when—" I stopped myself short when the queen glared so hard at me I was surprised I didn't go up in smoke immediately. "... Er, that is to say that, I arrived just this morning." I felt the eye roll from Phillipa across the room, right along with the panic.

"Did you—" The queen put her hand over her mouth. "Did you two—" Oh hell, she looked like she was ready to faint. Her jaw worked. Oh good, she was going to try speaking again without passing out. "Were you two in here? Alone?"

"No?" I offered lamely.

Phillipa covered her face with her hands. "Mother, it's not what you think. Besides, we're about to be married."

Her head whipped around so fast I got dizzy. "You mean you *wish* to marry… him? Truly?"

"I'm confused." I raised my hand. "Wasn't that the plan?"

"Well, yes." The queen nodded coolly. "You just weren't our first choice."

I winced.

"Or hers," she added.

"My ego feels fine, thanks," I muttered under my breath.

"He's mine," Phillipa piped up, her eyes widening right along with her declaration. "I mean, it's him or nobody."

I could have kissed her.

Would have launched myself at her had the queen not stared us down with a smile that was way too knowing for my liking. "Fantastic!"

"Wait." I held up my hand. "You just said—"

"I know my daughter." She shot me a glare. "Amazing what a little jealousy will do, and dear, you'll be happy to know I was lying. Melly let it slip that Fitz hadn't wandered out of your room yet." She cleared her throat. "By the way, you have no choice but to get married now that you've anticipated your vows and—"

"Actually…" I didn't want her mother to think the worst of Phillipa.

"Shut up, Fitz," Phillipa interjected.

Stunned, I stared at her in awe. Did the woman just silence me? Did I just like it? I was going to defend her honor and she told me to shut up?

"It's for the best then, since we've done just that," Phillipa lied, this time, well.

Had something happened while I wasn't even aware of it? How much did we drink? Hardly anything if I remember correctly.

"Well then, that's that." The queen reached for the door. "Come, Fitz, just because you spent the night doesn't mean you get to spend the day gawking."

"I wasn't gawking."

She flashed me a knowing smile. "You've always gawked."

"Son of a bitch," I muttered under my breath. Did everyone know about my fascination with Phillipa?

"To be fair," the queen added with a wink, "so has she."

Elated, I shared a smile with the queen and then one with Phillipa, whose face was so red you'd think she'd just gotten done with a marathon.

"Oh…" the queen interrupted my study of Phillipa's blush. "Do change into something that shouldn't be burned." She eyed my joggers and tight workout shirt. "This is…" Waving her hand in my general direction, she made a face.

I followed after her, then stopped, turned on my heel, and grabbed Phillipa's hand, pressing a kiss to the center of her wrist. "Princess."

She sighed breathlessly. "I still hate you, you know."

"Wouldn't be the same without all your hate."

"What wouldn't be the same?"

"True love's kiss." I grinned in anticipation as her breath quickened like she couldn't wait for more kissing, for more of me.

And if I was being honest, I couldn't wait either.

For the first time in my life, she was mine, I was hers. And I wasn't letting go.

CHAPTER TWELVE

Phillipa

I PRAYED FOR rescue.

I hadn't seen Fitz all day, and we had a diplomat dinner that I wasn't prepared for at all. Nor did I want to attend.

I would sit at the head of the table with my mother.

We'd smile and welcome the guests.

Talk business.

Drink expensive champagne and wine.

And I would be bored to tears.

On top of that, I was almost always asked how I was supposed to rule without a man by my side—by the very men who would rather golf than do their own duty.

It was so backwards.

Why not ask me how it was going to be different? How I'd like to cause change in a country that desperately needed it?

Our roads were fine, but we had just broken ground on

a new children's hospital and needed donations; I would be surprised if they were even aware we needed them!

To make matters worse, I'd lied to my mother about what had transpired between me and Fitz, leading her to give me an hour-long lecture on safe sex.

Or as she stated it, safe procreation for the realm.

Literally, word for word, that's how the conversation started.

Her sex talks could kill a person's libido on the spot.

I put on some creamy red lipstick and donned my black gloves. They went all the way past my elbows, and the silk felt smooth against my skin.

Plus, they matched the white and black gown perfectly. I rarely wore strapless dresses to dinners, mainly because I didn't want to constantly be tugging the dress up, and this one was heavier than most. This time, I used double-sided tape and hoped for the best.

This time, I wanted to look my best.

For him.

I adjusted my small tiara in the mirror and then very slowly made my way to the door and opened it.

Fitz was standing there, waiting, his smile wide, his massive shoulders tucked into a black tuxedo jacket with all of his medals hanging on the left-hand side. The guy had enough royal decorations on the front lapel of his coat to make a person go blind.

I used to hate it.

It always felt like he was bragging.

Tonight, however, I felt proud.

"Here's a thought." He leaned in and put his hands on my hips, drawing me closer to him. "We pretend we're both sick and lock the door to your bedroom. If I turn up Hallmark really loud, they'll just think we're in the holiday mood."

"Which we would be…" I smiled, loving the warmth from his body. "If we were watching Hallmark instead of eating a boring dinner."

"I don't believe I said anything about watching the TV." He tapped my nose and then brushed a kiss across my lips, so soft I almost didn't feel it. "Doubtful I would be able to keep my hands off of you this time."

"And last time?"

"I was being a gentleman."

"What changed?" I hooked my arm in his as we started walking.

"Everything," he whispered under his breath. "Besides, I've suddenly discovered there's no fun in people assuming we've done anything when I haven't even gotten the chance to seduce you."

I tripped in my heels and then scowled up at him. "What makes you think I'm so easy to seduce?"

"Easy? No, never. I've waited years for you to even smile at me. It won't be easy, but I think I'd enjoy the journey and all the many tries before you finally give in."

"Which I won't."

"But you could," he said in an optimistic tone. "One friend to another?"

I burst out laughing. "You're impossible!"

"That's why you like me. Plus, admit it, you're relieved you don't have to sit by yourself while Lord Andrey goes on and on and on about his potato farm."

"He's made me hate potatoes, and I've always loved fries. So depressing."

"Hmm, I can't argue with you there. Last time I had mashed potatoes, all I kept seeing was him fishing for something in his nose, wiping it down his shirt, and then going, 'Now where were we?' before going back into a lecture on ways to boil them without losing all that flavor."

I covered my laugh with my glove as we turned the corner and made our entrance down the grand staircase.

Men and women—important men and women—were littered around the expansive and festively decorated room, champagne glasses in hand.

Fitz and I stopped for the announcement. "Her Royal Highness the Princess of Answorth, and her fiancé, the Royal Duke of Belleville."

A chill ran down my spine. A chill of excitement, of thoughts of our future. Kids. I gulped and looked up at Fitz.

He had a funny expression on his face before he leaned down and pressed another feather-soft kiss to my lips.

We touched foreheads. I wanted to cherish the moment of solidarity, the moment when we were announced as a couple.

The moment I suddenly stopped feeling so alone.

The moment I felt like I'd finally stopped grieving my father.

"Shall we?" His voice suddenly sounded different to me, grittier, sexier.

"We shall." I beamed as people clapped around us.

Maybe it was the kiss or maybe the smiles on both our faces. It felt like, finally, pieces were falling into place.

And then Fitz whispered in my ear, "Not it."

"What?"

"Princess Phillipa!" Lord Andrey grasped my hands. "Did you know I just found the neatest recipe for potato pie?"

I glared at Fitz's back, noticed the movement of laughter, and mentally strangled him until he apologized, all while smiling at Lord Andrey and nodding my head. "Lovely."

"Now, the trick is—"

I drowned him out for at least a minute, nodding, smiling, and trying not to look bored out of my mind.

Rescue came another eternity later when my mother stopped to compliment my dress and the obvious happiness on my face.

Great, she probably thought it was because of what didn't happen with Fitz. When, instead, it was because I was genuinely happy with him by my side.

Where was he?

I scanned the room just in time to see France's diplomat and his wife talking with him.

The wife touched Fitz's shoulder suggestively, right in front of her husband.

Stunned, I watched as Fitz stiffened and moved farther away.

Why did it matter that other women, even married women, gave him attention? I hated that I was instantly jealous.

"Excuse me," I said my apologies to my mother who was now trapped with Andrey and weaved my way through the crowd to Fitz. "There you are!"

He turned and sighed in relief. "My love."

I leaned in and kissed his cheek, then whispered in his ear, "Payback's a bi—"

"Phillipa." He coughed before I could finish. "May I introduce one of my favorite diplomats from France, Charles Berling, the Baron of Hastings, and his wife, Baroness Marie of Hastings."

They both bowed.

I smiled warmly at the baron and then turned my attention to the baroness, who was already sizing me up and finding me wanting.

Her loss.

Fitz wrapped an arm around me. "Now, you look like you could use some more champagne, my love." He winked. "Let's go find some before dinner."

"It was lovely meeting you." I eyed both of them, lingering on the baroness, letting her know I was perfectly aware that she was attracted to Fitz.

Then again, who wouldn't be?

"You're tense," he murmured in my ear as a waiter passed with a tray.

"I really miss Hallmark right now."

"I really miss your bed right now. With you in it, of course, not snoring like you did the night before, but—"

I elbowed him, nearly spilling my own champagne. "I did not snore!"

"You did." His grin was too beautiful to process. "I took pictures and a video for the next time I do something wrong and need to blackmail you."

"And are you planning on doing something wrong?"

"No, it's just a natural occurrence where you're concerned. I like to be prepared. Love is warfare after all." He sipped his wine, choked a bit, and then looked away.

"Love, hmm?" My voice was shaky. "Are you saying you love me?"

"I'm saying you're lovable, and I can see myself very easily getting seduced by the way you smell, and don't even get me started on that dress. Is that legal? That much skin showing?"

He ran his hand from my shoulder down my collarbone.

I cleared my throat in warning.

"What?"

"People will see."

"Then let them see that I can't keep my hands off my future wife," he growled possessively.

I swallowed against my dry throat. "You can't say things that you don't mean, Fitz."

"I do mean it." The words tumbled out of his mouth. "My only warning is this: if you don't lock your door tonight, I'm going to assume it's an invitation."

"For a tryst?"

"Perhaps." He seemed amused. "Or maybe I just want to document more snoring for my own evil purposes."

I rolled my eyes.

"Dinner is served!" our butler, Harold, announced loud enough for the country next door to hear. Then again, he was so hard of hearing he felt the need to yell everything, but at least we never missed a meal!

Fitz escorted me behind Mother.

I was already bored and not really paying attention to anything except for eating like a lady (not too fast, not too slow), answering questions in between sips of wine, and trying not to feel the heat emanating from Fitz's thigh as it brushed against mine several times.

I almost choked on a brussels sprout when his hand landed on my thigh.

He continued talking to my mother as if nothing was out of the ordinary, as if he wasn't pressing his palm against my dress suggestively under the table.

"Darling, are you okay?" My mother angled her head,

eyebrows raised in query.

"Wrong tube," I said with a rasp, reaching for more wine just as Fitz squeezed my thigh again.

Was it possible to feel someone's touch everywhere?

I felt his.

I wanted more.

I was having trouble thinking straight.

My pulse was pounding uncontrollably.

"So, Your Highness..." Lady Hastings's sly tone had me jerking my head in her direction. "We're all so elated at your upcoming marriage. In fact, it was such a surprise to all of us I don't believe anyone truly knows how it all came about."

Fear trickled down my spine.

If they knew it was completely arranged then they'd doubt my ability. What type of woman can't even land her own man? A queen, no less.

And I knew my reputation.

I knew what was whispered behind my back.

About my duty to the crown.

There was a horrible blog post last year that had a cartoon of me sitting on the throne in my nineties with a dozen cats and droopy breasts accompanied by the caption, *"Why does nobody love me?"*

I was horrified.

And angry. So, so angry.

Because what if it was true?

"Well..." I paused so I could think of something believable.

"Actually," Fitz interrupted softly. "I doubt she'll tell you the real story, so I'll do the honors."

Unease filled my lungs until it was hard to breathe.

"Candy canes," Fitz announced.

The table erupted in soft laughter.

"She tried killing me with a candy cane when we were kids. She was upset over me going into the Christmas Ball and her not getting to go because of her age, and I knew right then and there that one day I would marry her. And every year after that she grew more beautiful, more wise, more terrifying."

My mother joined in on laughing now, but it was with amusement, with love. Tears welled in my eyes. Why was he being so devoted? Why had he changed the story? And who knew he could lie so well?

"And I did things to garner her attention—stupid things, because I preferred her attention even if it meant she hated me, and hate me she did—"

"Until he opened my eyes," I said softly, "to a world of friendship and desire, to the world of a partnership I had only ever wished for in my dreams."

Lady Hastings's face fanned red.

Take that.

"Same." Fitz lifted my gloved hand and kissed the back of it. "But enough about us. How did you meet your husband, Baroness? It wasn't one of those boring marriage betrothals between families, was it?"

Mother choked on her sip of wine while I tried not to burst out laughing, because from the looks of every uncomfortable face in the room, it had been exactly that.

"Oh…" Fitz made a face. "I didn't mean to insult; I had no idea. The lovely news is you both look very much in love. How lucky for you." He lifted his glass into the air. "To the Baroness of Hastings and her lucky husband."

It wasn't lost on me that the aging diplomat looked anything but thankful or lucky as he raised his glass, expression grim.

I fell in love a little bit more as I leaned in and kissed Fitz on the cheek.

"What was that for?" he whispered as conversation continued around the table.

"For being you." I sighed happily.

"Princess," he rasped. "You can look at me like that all you want, but I'm still not sending you the video of you snoring."

I glared.

"You'll have to do more than kiss me on the cheek."

Two could play that game.

I leaned in and whispered under my breath, "I think I'll take that challenge."

"Oh, hell," he muttered, gripping his napkin like it was going to keep him from gripping me.

"Dessert!" Harold announced loudly, making both me and Fitz jump, and I knew by the expression on his face he wasn't thinking about the soufflé being served.

CHAPTER THIRTEEN

Fitz

I PACED IN front of her door.

Like a madman.

Was it locked?

Unlocked?

Would I break it down if it were locked and wake up the entire castle, both mothers included?

Yes. Yes, I would.

I quietly turned the knob, relieved it was open, and then hurriedly stepped through the opening and shut the door behind me.

The room was blanketed in darkness except for the sliver of moon peeking out through the drapes.

And there she was.

My princess.

My future wife.

In bed, watching Hallmark.

Again.

She sat up as I walked toward her, wordlessly moving my heavier weight onto the mattress and pulling her into my arms.

"Is this you trying to seduce me?" She sighed with contentment.

"If I was seducing you, you'd know, trust me. In fact, the entire castle would probably know, including the horses, cows, ducks—"

"I get the point." She laughed and tilted her head up at me.

Our mouths were close. I just wanted to close the distance and hold on forever.

"You're a man of many words. I was just curious if you use your quick wit to seduce first and your sex appeal second, or vice versa."

"Sex appeal." I laughed. "It's strange. I simply take off my shirt, the end."

"Good story." She kissed my chin. "Does it have a happy ending?"

"Then? No, never. Those endings always included me jumping out windows and sneaking away with one shoe. Besides, that's in the past. Remember my talk with your father? I'd like to think I've been on my best behavior since then."

"So you really haven't…" she pried, her eyes narrowing, "…been with anyone since then?"

"You." I tucked her hair behind her ear. "Just you."

She let out a shaky exhale and then kissed me with what felt like years of pent up passion. Not one to argue with a woman who clearly knew her own mind, I kissed her back like I wished I could every day I saw her when she scowled at me, every day she said something menacing or tried to trip me.

I kissed her with years of feelings, with my whole heart on my sleeve, with my body aching for her in ways I didn't even understand were possible.

"Fitz." She lifted my shirt over my head and tossed it.

"Yes?" I tugged at her lips with my teeth, then slid my tongue into her mouth, pulling her close.

"If you ever…" She panted between kisses. "And I do mean ever…" Damn, her hands were fast working when she wanted something. They roamed over my abs and gripped my shoulders with purpose. "*Ever…*" she repeated for a third time. "Cheat on me…"

I almost laughed at her aggression—almost.

"…I will castrate you and let wolves feed on your bloody beaten body, clear?"

"Crystal." I swallowed a laugh as our eyes locked. Damn, she was beautiful. "Something you should know about me, Princess."

Her features softened.

"When I find a treasure… I hoard it."

"Ah, and that's your flaw, hoarding."

"At least I can admit it. I'm like a raccoon. I like really pretty, shiny things. But with even more beautiful hearts, I like to keep those things close."

Her smile lit up her entire face. "You really need to start writing the prime minister's speeches."

"Hrmph. Bastard won't let me anymore. He got jealous that the media only gave attention to the ones I wrote." I shrugged.

Her eyes widened. "You aren't kidding, are you?"

"Not in the slightest." I kissed her again. "Now, can we stop talking about Eugene and kiss already?"

"His name is Eu—"

"Shhhh…" I kissed the question away. "Middle name, yes, and he hates to be called that. Now, shut up and kiss me."

She did.

And I dug my hands into her hair, then grabbed her by the hips and flipped her onto her back, hovering over her as I kissed, and tasted, and dreamed of a night like this one when she'd be mine.

"I can't get enough of you, of this," she gasped as I kissed her at a different angle, trying to decipher what she liked best, changing pressure and speed, only to change it again because everything was so new, and excited because we had time.

"Me neither," I agreed, pulling back.

Her lips were swollen, her shirt had ridden up, and she looked thoroughly seduced even though we'd only kissed like teenagers.

"Why are you stopping?" She looked ready to pout.

"Because of your father," I admitted quickly. "All I can see is that damn shovel and all the snow I saved from heavy boots and heels." I groaned and covered my face with my hands. "Swear his words are haunting me. I want nothing more than to strip you down and show you all the ways you'll be screaming 'your majesty' in bed, but…" I sighed, hating myself. "I have a vow to keep, and I don't think he would be happy with me if I just spent the next eight days finding ways to make you scream in pleasure. Don't get me wrong, it sounds like the best idea I've ever had, I just— You deserve all the perfect moments, not the rushed frantic kisses—though those are bloody incredible too. You know, I'm just going to go before I talk myself out of being a gentleman to the future queen."

"Wife first," she said softly. "Queen second."

I stared her down. Her hair was messy around her shoulders, her lips bee-stung, her eyes so damn seductive that I had to look away. "You will always be my wife first, my queen second. I couldn't bear to have it any other way."

She reached for me.

I kissed the back of her hand. "If you'll excuse me, I have a date with a very cold shower."

"There's always snow!" she called after me.

I glared. "If I find snow anywhere near any region below my neck while I'm sleeping, I'm going to post the snoring picture on Instagram."

"But you have like twenty million followers!"

"Aw, been stalking me, Princess?"

A pillow flew by my face.

It missed me.

I laughed. "I deserved that. Sleep well!"

"Dream of me while you shower," she quipped.

"Not at all helpful," I said in a sing-song voice as I shut the door behind me and came face to face with the queen. "I was just checking… for… rats."

And I was the good liar of the two of us. Incredible.

"Are you under the assumption that we have a rat problem here at the castle, Your Grace?"

"Not at all. I'm just protective." I grinned wolfishly.

"Uh-huh. Well, be sure to be protective of more than just a rat attack. You still have eight full days before you say, 'I do.'"

"I have a countdown, similar to the Christmas chain in the hall, only mine's made out of con—"

"Fitz, really!" The queen blushed.

"What?" I grinned. "I was going to say confessions of her beauty. Whatever did you think I was going to say?"

The glare she subjected me to was quite reminiscent of her daughter's.

I deserved to be slapped, probably, but there it was.

"Have you read through what I gave you?" She put her hands on her hips, her voice lowered. "From my…" Her eyes filled with tears. "From the late king?"

"Some of it, yes."

"Good." She seemed uncertain that it was good. "Have you told Phillipa yet?"

"No, I did as you said, though I need to tell her soon, I want no secrets between us."

"I've given it some thought, her father and she were very close. I think it might offer her some comfort to know that, even in his grave, he's here with her, guiding her… and you." She sighed. "A word of caution, be sure to read everything before you decide."

Fear trickled down my spine. "I'll finish reading tonight and be sure to show her tomorrow."

"Very well." She nodded. "Good evening, Your Grace."

"Your Majesty." I bowed and watched her go, then slowly walked to my room.

I knew sleep wouldn't come anytime soon, so I made sure to go to my desk and pull open the folder with the rest of the notes from the king.

Most of them were orders to allow the future queen to rule as she saw fit.

Which was a given.

He included some of her favorite poetry and songs that could be used for the ceremony, which I knew she would appreciate.

And the final piece of paper was a note to Phillipa.

If the queen didn't want me to read it, she wouldn't have left it in there, so I picked it up and read.

My Dear Phillipa,

If you're reading this, I've since passed. Know that I love you with all of my heart, and I am there with you even now as you marry the man of your dreams.

I know you will choose wisely.

I know he will be perfect for the crown despite his many, many, numerous, outstanding flaws. Perfection is never in the completion of tasks or making sure that every choice is right. It's in trying your hardest every day, like I know both of you will attempt to do.

You never did see the signs, and I would hate to think my death would make it so you isolate yourself even more than you already do.

This man, the one of my choosing, has no idea I'm writing this. In fact, I think he'd probably burn it so you wouldn't find it, but he is the sort of man who pulls you from your shell.

He challenges and provokes you.

If you read this, that means my dream has come true for your future and you are currently engaged to marry Fitz.

If not, then I gather your mother will blot out half of this letter and tell you felicitations are in order.

Now, Fitz, stop reading. You always were such a snoop. And remember to love my daughter well, without restraint, and with purpose each and every day. And Phillipa, love him back with what I believe is the biggest heart I've had the opportunity to hold.

I hereby give you my blessing.

Live full.

Live well.

Your father.

He had known!

How?

How had he known? Had he always been that perceptive? And what would Phillipa think if she knew that this was ordained during all the hateful years where we tried killing one another?

I wiped my hands down my face. Maybe it would give her peace? Or maybe it would make her feel controlled even from the grave.

I groaned. This one piece of paper could possibly ruin everything, because even though we were being forced together, I'd like to think she now at least had chosen it.

What if she knew her father's greatest wish was coming true? It could go either way, and I hated that I wasn't sure which way that would be: for me or against me.

Suddenly exhausted, I tucked the letter back into the folder and went in search of a shower while my thoughts followed me and haunted me well into my sleep.

CHAPTER FOURTEEN

Phillipa

I KNEW SOMETHING was wrong the minute someone was furiously knocking on my door at five in the morning.

I jolted out of bed, nearly taking my sheets with me, and quickly opened the door to see a frantic-looking Harold.

"Your mother's fine," he said in a still-worried voice. "However…"

I braced for whatever he was going to say next.

"She's been violently ill all night and can't attend any of the events today, and starting in two hours, she was hosting a breakfast at the orphanage, followed by a meeting with—"

"I know her schedule," I said in a tired voice. "I'll do whatever needs to be done."

He exhaled in relief. "Good, perfect."

"I'll get ready as fast as I can. Please have some coffee and breakfast sent up as soon as possible."

"Right away, Your Highness." He bowed and then half walked, half skipped down the hall like a man on a mission.

I closed the door and leaned against it. For the first time in my life, I resented having to do something good, like feed the orphans.

I resented it all.

Because I could still taste Fitz on my lips.

Loneliness seeped into my bones. Would I be the sort of queen that was always doing everything for everyone? Missing Fitz? Wondering what he was doing?

I quickly got dressed in a white Gucci number with a fur coat and my diamond earrings. I straightened my hair and made sure I had no flyaways, and then sipped my coffee before putting on a pair of camel-colored boots over my tan nylons.

Taking one last look in the mirror, I grabbed my purse and opened the door.

"Ready?" Fitz had his arm out.

I stared wide-eyed at his arm like it was a plague, then looked up at him in confusion. "I can't today, Fitz. Mother's ill, and I need to help and—" Why was I getting emotional?

"I know." His smile was warm, protective. "My mother woke me up panicking that we weren't going to have all the wedding details planned in time. Not sure why she's so concerned, as it's our wedding. I just want to be with you."

It was the sweetest thing he'd ever said to me.

"Me too." My eyes filled with tears.

"None of that." He kissed the top of my head. "I'll ride with you to every function, smile, shake hands, and in our free time—of which we have barely any today—we'll take a look through this." He held up a book. "Just a few rules of the royal wedding we have to follow, which we get to agree or disagree with, nothing crazy."

"Okay." I nodded. "Okay, that works, right? We'll be fine. It's just a busy day and—"

"Phillipa." He braced me by the shoulders. "Breathe, that's it, inhale, exhale."

I leaned against him and used his strength as my own.

"You were born to do this, Princess. All you need to do is exist and let your body default, all right?"

"Thank you." I clung to him tightly. "For being you."

"Of course." He winked and then slipped a candy cane into my purse.

I smiled the entire drive to the orphanage.

We were a hit.

Fitz told stories to the children. They were in love with him instantly, and I began to wonder if I hadn't always been just a little bit in love with him my whole life.

The day went by in a blur of duty and wedding planning, and by the time we were back at the castle, we were both exhausted and ready for bed.

Mother was better but couldn't be disturbed. She didn't want either of us to get sick, which was ridiculous, but we did learn that the following day would be even busier, and the one after that as well.

Six days later and both Fitz and I had spent every waking moment at meetings, dinner parties, luncheons… the list went on.

More and more we settled into a routine. We had breakfast in my room while I finished getting ready because I was always running two minutes late. He read the paper out loud so I knew what was going on in the country. We shared pastries, and he stole my bacon.

Every. Morning.

He was kind enough to eat any fish that came across my plate, and I was kind enough to steal anything chocolate that was given to him, including dinner mints.

It was so natural, being with him, that I didn't even realize we'd begun to finish each other's sentences in public, something we did often in private.

We had two days before the wedding, and we hadn't had any time to just be us. Between picking out my own dress that didn't offend the crown, and my duties during the day, we were both completely swamped, either working together on the country or working apart on our impending nuptials.

It was beginning to drive me crazy.

It didn't help that he touched me all the time, kissed my cheek like he was made for it, and never let go of my hand.

I wanted more.

Craved it.

I was past the point of being desperate—way past—especially since I'd had a vivid daydream about shoving him into one of the hall closets and ripping his shirt from his body.

Something that made me smile more than it should during diplomatic meetings about our country's national security.

The day was finally coming to a close, and I was so exhausted I just naturally laid my head on Fitz's shoulder as our driver took us back toward the castle.

It was starting to snow again, something that made the world feel magical, like we were in our own personal snow globe.

"I can feel you smiling," Fitz said, the rasp of his tired voice more prevalent than usual this evening. Then again, he was doing a lot of public speaking, a lot of charming the pants off of people, and the newspapers didn't lie.

The entire country was enraptured with our love story.

The only thing missing was the actual declaration of love.

I was too afraid to tell him I was falling.

Too afraid he wouldn't catch me.

I was my own cliché.

A strong independent woman who didn't need a man but who desperately wanted to love one.

I'd lived my life shouting my independence, and at the first taste of a partnership, I felt like a woman who'd been starved her whole life.

It wasn't just the romance.

It was that I actually had a friend, too. Someone to share the burden. Someone I could be myself with.

"It's snowing," I said softly.

"I figured you were smiling because we're almost home and we get to watch another one of your favorite movies with our sweats on and freshly baked Christmas cookies." A small chuckle rumbled out. "I think a wine pairing is in order, don't you?"

I laughed against his shoulder and pressed my left hand to his chest. He grabbed my fingers and kissed them while my stomach did somersaults.

I wanted more than cookies and wine.

More than my romantic movies.

"Don't lie, you shed a tear last night."

"I had a sprinkle in my eye, and I'll deny any tears to my grave."

"The whole following her on horseback and then declaring his love was a nice touch."

"And," he added, "it started snowing. Classic."

"It's romantic, like kissing in the rain," I argued. "Except better because it's Christmas."

"Hmmm."

"Uh oh, I know what that hmmm means. You're thinking too hard again, aren't you? We can't have you spraining brain cells before you have to read your vows."

"My brain cells are fine, as you well know. I think I should be nominated for an award for that speech downtown today."

I pinched him in the side.

"Ow!"

"Fine, it's true, but humility, Fitz, say it with me, humility."

"I don't understand what you're talking about." He kissed the top of my head and sighed like he was finally relaxed.

The car pulled around and up to the front door.

I was distracted with grabbing my purse and tossing my cell phone in it and almost smacked into Fitz's waiting hand as he helped me out of the car.

Instead of walking with me, he pulled me against his chest. "Romantic, hmm?"

I chewed my lower lip. "What are you doing?"

"Being romantic," came his answer before he dipped his head and kissed me soundly on the mouth. I gasped at the heat of his lips, the velvet touch of his tongue, and the way I couldn't get close enough even when we had no space separating us whatsoever.

Snowflakes kissed my cheeks while he kissed my mouth.

It was heaven.

He made a growling noise as he tilted my chin and angled his head to the side like he, too, needed to deepen the kiss even though it was probably impossible.

I liked his kisses better than snow.

Better than my movies.

Better than anything.

They both calmed and lit a fire within me.

"Ahem," a throat cleared nearby.

Fitz didn't stop right away.

I clung to the front of his lapels.

And then he finally pulled back and kissed my forehead before turning his head to the side. "Yes, Mother?"

"Sorry for the interruption." She looked anything but sorry and actually a little smug. "Did you two have a chance to write your vows? We're forty-eight hours away from the wedding, twenty-four hours away from the rehearsal."

"You can count," Fitz commented with a gleam in his eyes.

His mother scowled. "Remember who brought you into this world."

"God."

I moaned into my hands while his mother gave me a look that said, *He's your problem now.*

"We'll finish them tonight," I piped up and then rubbed his back smoothly with my hand.

He relaxed into me and nodded his head.

"Lovely." She smiled at both of us. "Must say, this worked out quite well, didn't it?"

"You see where I get my smug demeanor," Fitz whispered under his breath while I let out a laugh, knowing full well the duchess heard what he said.

She just rolled her eyes heavenward and went back into the castle while we slowly followed.

"So…" Fitz looked suddenly nervous. "Shall I persuade the staff to deliver food and wine to your room or mine?"

I perked up. "Yours."

"Wow, eager to be in my bed?"

"You've been saving that response for at least two days, haven't you?"

"Three." He grinned. "Go get changed. I'll take care of everything, Princess."

I watched him go.

And all I could think was, *I know*.

I trusted him implicitly.

With everything.

With my heart.

My soul.

My country.

What a terrifying truth.

CHAPTER FIFTEEN

Fitz

TRUTH? I WAS exhausted.

Truth? I wasn't used to faking so many smiles in so many hours. It was a tiring existence. I'd feel weak, and then I'd reach for Phillipa's hand, and all of a sudden, the strength was back. Yes, I could do one more meeting. Yes, I could pull another speech out of my ass.

We worked together seamlessly.

It was terrifying.

To think that my entire life she'd been right under my nose, and I'd held too many grudges against her to realize we were the perfect match.

Opposites, and yet, the same.

Her father had known it.

He'd also known we needed time—at least I'd like to think that.

I was still distressed over the fact that he'd chosen me, distressed that she would take it wrong, and then, on days like this, I told myself I was being ridiculous because there was no sure way she would have chosen me.

He gave her the option to choose until all of the men ran away screaming, except for me.

So maybe the late king just knew his daughter that well.

It was a mystery and would continue to be. I needed to tell her tonight, before she found out somehow without me. The last thing I needed was her assuming that I was hiding something from her.

I informed the kitchen staff to bring wine and refreshments to the room along with some of the freshly baked cookies. Then, I took the stairs two at a time and jogged into my room.

It was dark.

And tempting.

I wanted nothing more than to sit in that room, watch a movie, and fall asleep with her in my arms.

Instead, I backed out of the very tempting room and turned just in time to see Phillipa making her way toward me, smile wide. "Are you going to stand outside your room or actually go in?"

"I went in. This is me coming back out."

Her face fell.

I reached for her. "I had a thought."

"Seems my warnings about thinking too hard are going unnoticed," she grumbled against my chest.

"It's been a busy day, and I know you're exhausted. Why don't I draw you a bath?"

She relaxed against me.

"While I sit on the other side of the room, writing my

vows. We can write them together, get them finished."

"Oh!" Melly pushed a cart toward us. "I was told to bring this up. Were you leaving?"

Phillipa leaned up on her tiptoes and whispered in my ear. "I'll take a bath in your bathroom. The tub there's my favorite anyway. I used to hide in it when I was small."

"I know, because I found you at least a dozen times with your eyes closed and your ears plugged."

"My knight." She smirked.

"Something like that." I grinned right back and then motioned for Melly to bring the cart into the room while I went and started to draw a bath in the adjoining room. The guest rooms at the castle were like apartments, big enough to house a small family.

Mine was smaller than most, but I'd always preferred staying closer to her.

Something I always claimed was because I wanted to keep my eye on her in case she tried to kill me in my sleep.

The feeling I was now recognizing as a need to just be near her even if I was the object of her hate.

I tested the water and let the tub fill, then turned and collided with Phillipa. I steadied her with my hands and swallowed slowly as she licked her lips.

There was so much in that stare that I wanted to dissect, to discuss, to kiss away.

Instead, I smiled briefly and moved out of the way. "I'll get you some wine or champagne, whatever they sent up."

Hands shaking, I went over to the cart. Melly had already left, which was good. It gave me time to get my feelings under control.

This woman. God, this woman.

I wanted her.

Not just for one night, for forever.

And I hadn't realized until that moment how lacking I was for self-control. I just wanted to react. I was a man of action, and it was like my heart demanded I do exactly that. Take action. Make her mine.

I turned and brought the chilled white wine back into the bathroom just in time for Phillipa to turn off the water and face me. "Thanks." She took a sip of the wine I'd put on the counter and then peeled her hoodie over her head.

Thank God, she was wearing a tank top.

I stared when I should have looked away, and I'd like to think she knew I was watching and needed more, needed to satisfy something within me.

Slowly, she reached for the bottom of her tank top and lifted, lifted, lifted, until it was over her head and all she was wearing was a black sports bra. A logical person would deduce that it covered more than most bikinis, but I wasn't feeling very logical. I was feeling damned aroused.

In all my wildest fantasies.

I hadn't imagined her.

Like this.

My eyelids grew heavy, almost like I was in a trance, as I watched her sit and slowly roll down her leggings. I almost choked when she stood to face me.

Matching black lacy something that made me feel like I was going to pass out if I couldn't touch her skin.

"This is the part where you leave." A sweet smile curved her lips.

"I think we should re-write this part. It's terrible, the leaving part. After all, leaving's always associated with sadness, and I'm not feeling particularly sad right now, but I will be if you stop."

"You really are so good with words, Fitz." She laughed. "Go grab a pen. I can hear you from the sitting room if you want to talk about our vows. And remember, this was your idea."

"Clearly I'm an idiot, and this is why you're going to rule the country," I grumbled. "Worst idea I've ever had, and I've had a lot of them."

"I made a list," she agreed. "Laminated it on both sides."

"Of course you did." I smirked, grabbed my glass, took one last look at the woman who would soon be mine, then cursed under my breath and went into the sitting room.

The fire in the hearth roared in front of me.

I tortured myself with images of her taking every scrap of clothing off and dangling it on one finger before pulling me against her.

Instead, I heard water.

A long, blissful sigh.

And nearly spontaneously combusted.

With a sad, regretful little sigh, I grabbed my blank sheet of paper and wrote "Vows" at the top, then stared at the word while I tapped my pen.

"Are you stuck?" she called out, splashing water around.

I grinned, chaotic even when she bathed. "Maybe."

A small sigh of resignation came from the bathroom. "Start with the truth."

"Come again?"

"Truth."

Five minutes passed, then ten. The splashing stopped, and that's when I started writing: my truth, our truth, our love.

"I started watching my future queen the day she tried to kill me," I admitted with a soft laugh. "I was teasing her, despite how much older I was, and I found it funny that this perfect pristine princess I would one day call queen was so irritated over missing a ball of all things. She used her candy cane as a weapon, and that was the beginning of the end." I read the words out loud.

"Really?" Phillipa piped up, her voice full of emotion.

I didn't respond. I just kept writing and reading it to her.

"She is the only woman I want to kiss. The only woman I want to hold. My first choice in a fight. My first choice as a friend and lover. I vow to love you unconditionally, to stand by your side, even when I want to fight all your battles for you, to challenge you when you need it, to comfort you when you need comfort, and to hold your heart like the treasure it is. I vow to you not just my thoughts, my actions, my body. I vow to you my very soul."

A droplet of water fell onto the page I was hunched over. I looked up into Phillipa's eyes. She had a towel wrapped around her body, and a few water droplets were in the ends of her hair that had gotten wet. "Do you mean that?"

God, she was beautiful. So beautiful I sometimes forgot to breathe. "With all my heart."

She sat on my lap and pulled me in for a kiss. I gripped the left side of her hip, feeling nothing but towel and skin. She broke the kiss and stood directly in front of me as the flames from the fireplace seemed to flicker higher and higher.

The towel dropped to the floor.

"Are you seducing me?" I croaked, barely able to get the question out.

"Looks like it." She put her hands on her hips.

I nearly swallowed my tongue, and then I shot out from my chair and pulled her into my arms. I tasted the sweetness of the wine, and I devoured whatever she was going to say next as I shrugged out of my jacket. She hurriedly unbuttoned my shirt and jerked it open. Her hands were hot as she placed them across my abs and let out a little sigh of contentment.

"Been wanting to do that a while, hmmm?" I teased.

She smacked nothing but muscle then reached for me again. "Do you always have to tease?"

"With you, yes." I kissed her harder and pulled back. "Think of it as a sign of my devotion, of my obsession. If I don't tease you, I probably don't like you."

"It's good you're a mature adult now." She laughed then eagerly unbuttoned my slacks.

I kissed her and shrugged out of the rest of my clothes as I pressed her back against the mattress. "I've been wanting this since you got your eighteenth birthday present, admittedly sooner..."

She smiled against my mouth. "So you're saying I grew boobs and suddenly we should get naked?"

"The other present." I nipped her lower lip. "I wanted a ride in your flashy new car, maybe some making out in the back seat. I wanted to make you smile."

"I'm smiling now," she whispered with emotion.

"Oh, sweetheart, you're going to be doing more than smiling in a few seconds. Note that I say seconds, because I've been trying not to maul you for most of my adult life. Seems even when I hated you, a part of me wanted you, so damn much."

Her breath hitched as I kissed down her neck and showed her exactly what I meant by more than smiling. Then again, I was always really good with my hands and my mouth.

And it was her.

Phillipa.

"This is going to be—" She didn't let me finish. Instead, I just went with it like I always did with her, fighting, loving, arms and legs entwined. I finally had everything I'd always wanted.

It was us.

Together.

Her body clenched tightly around mine. I tried so desperately to slow down each thrust, to savor our closeness, but it was heaven, pure heaven.

She peppered little kisses on my chin. I had no idea a person could experience actual joy in sex.

Joy with the right person.

Joy with the person you were always meant to be with.

The treasure always in front of you.

"Princess," I growled when she gripped my ass. "If you want me to show you how impressive I can be in bed, you shouldn't do that…"

"Be impressive later." She bit down on my bottom lip. "Be mine now."

I didn't need any more encouragement.

And in the end, when we were both panting, both staring at one another in awe, I saw my life with that woman.

I saw my future.

And I knew I would do anything to keep her happy.

CHAPTER SIXTEEN

Phillipa

How could I have ever hated him?

Sure, he was annoying.

Prideful.

Ridiculously good looking.

Always out to best me at everything.

He was like the partner in crime I never wanted but had desperately needed my entire life.

He was also currently snoring.

Which only made him more endearing. Clearly, I was in love if I wasn't ready to shove a pillow over his face and hold it there until his legs stopped flopping around.

The sun was up.

Which meant we both needed to be up as well.

Duties and all.

In one day, I would be married, and tonight we would

have the rehearsal dinner at the cathedral.

Nerves attacked—not at what I was doing but what would happen afterwards. I would be crowned Queen.

At least I had him at my side.

I smiled again as I slowly got out of his bed and went in search of my clothes. I quickly changed in the bathroom, grabbed my shoes, and then accidentally bumped into one of the desks.

A few papers scattered to the floor along with a heavy manila envelope.

I flipped it over and stared in stunned disbelief. *"To My Daughter's Future Husband."*

Emotion clogged my throat as I read through each and every page. My father's handwriting was so beautiful; I'd always complimented him on it.

I traced a few letters with my fingertips and tried to keep the hot tears at bay as one by one they slid down my cheeks.

His first letter made me laugh.

And then I read through a few more—silly things like, "You better not kill her," and "This is your job as king. "

He would have no legal power, but he still had to do certain things for the crown. The idea made me want to both smile and throttle Fitz at the same time. Why hadn't he told me?

I got to the very last page, another letter.

With each word, I grew more and more anxious.

Until I saw it.

Fitz.

He'd always known it was Fitz?

But how?

Did Fitz know that?

Was there a betrothal between us that my mother lied

about? I flipped the page over, no more handwriting.

My father's dying wish was for me to marry Fitz.

And nobody, not even the man I loved, had let me in on that fact.

CHAPTER SEVENTEEN

Fitz

I WOKE UP to an empty room, an empty bed, and an empty heart. An empty bladder, however, I did not possess. I quickly went into the bathroom and noticed that Phillipa's clothes were gone. I was immediately irritated that we had to sleep in separate beds until the wedding.

One more night.

I could handle that.

Or I could sneak into her room after the rehearsal dinner. Better plan.

I laughed at myself and went over to my desk to gather all the papers. I'd forgotten to tell her the night before, but the more time we spent together, the more I realized I was being a complete idiot.

What we had was real.

Letters or no letters, nothing changed the fact that I loved her, that I would do anything for her, and I hoped she felt the same.

I grabbed the folder and frowned when a green sticky note was attached with the words, *"We need to talk."*

Now, no man wants to ever hear those words let alone see them on incriminating documents days before his wedding to the love of his life.

Panic seized my chest as I scrambled to get ready for the day and then made my way to Phillipa's room.

The door was closed.

"Princess?" I knocked twice. "It's Fitz."

"She's not there," Melly said as she passed me by with a giddy smile. "She's eating breakfast with your mother and the queen, and they are not to be disturbed."

"Not disturbed? Why?" A cold sweat broke out across my forehead as I waited for her to explain, something, anything.

She just shrugged. "How would I know what royalty discusses in private?"

"Right." I narrowed my eyes. "But if you did know, you would tell me, right?"

"I have a lot of work to do today, Your Grace." Her grin was the only hint that meant I wasn't going to be killed by my future wife.

I held onto that grin for the next hour.

And the hour after that.

And seven hours after that.

She avoided me at all costs.

The queen was still ailing, so she went straight to bed after breakfast—doctor's orders—and every time I tried to engage my own mother, she looked at me with indifference like I wasn't even her only son!

"Mother," I tried again four hours before the rehearsal dinner. "You don't understand; I need to talk to Phillipa. She's not answering my phone calls or texts. I can't find her anywhere."

"It's a day before the wedding. I sent her to the spa." She shrugged. "Why? Is that concerning to you?"

"Spa?" I repeated. "Which one?"

"The best one." She pulled a face of pure elation before waving me off. "I'll text you the directions, though she's probably already in for her waxing appointment."

My ears perked at that. "Why would she wax anything? She's perfect."

"And you would know that every outside inch of her is perfect because..." Her eyebrows shot up.

"Educated guess." I moved away just in case she tried swatting me with her hand, or pulling my ear, or yes, even kicking me in the nuts.

"Is it?"

"I better run." I sidestepped her and made a mad dash to the front of the castle. Mother had at least texted within seconds. "I need to go to Beau Monde, now."

The ride into town took ten minutes.

The car with its royal flags was, of course, noticeable, as was I, but I didn't care. I just needed to explain.

What if she felt angry? Betrayed? We couldn't start our marriage off like this; I wouldn't allow it.

"There," I yelled at the driver. "Wait for me, please."

I jogged to the spa, jerked the door open, and faced complete silence by at least seven different women, all in white coats, looking me up and down like I was on the menu for Christmas dinner.

"Uh, hi." I cleared my throat. "Is my fiancé by any chance here? I missed her this morning and had something important to discuss with her."

"Right this way," one lady said in a humored voice. "Your Grace, my name is Zelda. It's such an honor to have both of you here the day before your wedding. Now, your first treatment will include a special Japanese deep tissue massage. It's new."

"New?" I repeated. "Actually, I was just here to talk to—"

"We have you on the schedule. Both of you."

"That's odd."

"Not really." She beamed. "Right this way. Please discard all clothing, and your therapist will be with you in a moment."

"All right." What else was I supposed to do? I stripped naked and guessed at lying down face first and waited.

Ten minutes.

Finally, the door opened in and closed quickly, and the lights dimmed. I tried to relax even though I wanted to jump out of the room and run screaming down the halls.

"This may sting," the male voice said as something hot and oily was dropped onto my back.

My whole body tensed. Son of a…

"You okay?"

"Perfect," I said through clenched teeth as oil burned my skin in every direction. He spread it wide on my back, so light I could barely feel his fingers—not that I needed to feel his fingers, never mind.

It almost tickled.

Okay, it did tickle.

"Um, sir, could you please…" Oh dear God, please let this never leave this room. "Go harder?"

"Sir, are you asking me to go harder on you?"

"Yes, that would be great." I cringed so hard my face hurt.

"I like harder better too." He chuckled and then pushed a bit harder but nothing like a deep tissue. Again, it only tickled. What the hell was going on?

"Maybe, just a little…" I gulped. Kill me now. "Harder than that?"

"Would you like me to penetrate deeper, sir?"

Oh, hell. "Er, yes."

"Deep it is!" he announced, suddenly pressing what felt like his entire body weight onto me, my liver, spleen, and every other soft organ that was struggling for life. "Ready, Your Highness?"

"Highness?" I tried lifting my head, but the Vin Diesel of bodyguards shoved it back down in the hole while I started sweating profusely from tensing under his pressure.

"Guess we both have embarrassing videos now, hmmm?" came Phillipa's voice from behind me.

"Please tell me you don't have your cell phone," I begged.

Seconds later, she produced said cell phone under the donut hole where my face was and pressed play.

Naturally, it was me begging for bigger, better, harder, and my personal favorite, penetration.

Fantastic.

She paused when he slammed his body down onto mine and whispered, "My favorite part."

"Look, Phillipa, I know you're angry. Well, I'm assuming you're angry if you've resorted to pulling my mother into this just so you both can torture me into the next lifetime."

"Hmmm…" She paced in front of me; all I saw were her running shoes, pink and black. I loved them. I loved her. "And why would I be disappointed or angry?"

"Because I kept something from you. But you need to know. The queen gave it to me because I was marrying you. I only just finished reading everything a few nights ago and told her I'd tell you once I finished. I was going to tell you last night but, I got a little distracted, and if you need reminding of what happened last night, I'm more than willing to give a demonstration."

Her pacing stopped. "So you weren't going to keep it from me?"

"Never. But I will admit that at one point I didn't want you to see."

"Interesting. Why not?"

"Because…" The guy started shoving his elbow into my back, making it hard to breathe. "I had no idea he ever thought I was worthy of you, not that I am now as he's plainly scribbled over and over and over again, but I was terrified that you'd read that he knew and think it was just one more way you were getting told what to do, and I don't want to be part of that life. I don't want to be one more thing you have to do. Another duty, another responsibility." I shook my head slowly and sighed. "I just want you."

"Thomas, you can go," she announced quickly.

I shot up to see one of our mutual bodyguards making his way out of the small room with a giant grin on his face like he'd waited years to exact his revenge.

"Your bodyguard? Really?"

"I wasn't strong enough to torture you, so I called in a favor. Plus, you kind of deserved that after this bomb right before rehearsal." She crossed her arms.

"Phillipa, I'm sorry. God knows I'm sorry. What can I do to prove it to you?"

Her face lit up. "Ah, so the knight wants the lady's favor?"

I angled my head. "Funny… thought I already had it."

"My biggest fear…" Her face paled a bit. "…has always been being untruthful. No lies, Fitz, not between us. So if you have anything to say to me, say it now."

I reached for her, thankful that she let me touch her, and wrapped my arms around her. The only thing separating us was the thin sheet wrapped around my lower half.

"You want all the lies I've ever told concerning you? Here goes: I don't want her. I hate her. I loathe her. I'm not attracted to her. I don't want her to smile at me. I don't live for her laughs. I don't count down the days to every dinner party or event. I don't dream of her at night. I don't wish for her kiss. I don't wish for her love. I don't need her love. I don't need her. I'm perfectly fine just as I am—"

She interrupted me with a kiss. I smiled against her lips. "I could go on and on and on, because my entire life has been a lie. You're the only real true thing in it, because you're you, my love, and when you find your love, you suddenly realize that's your life too. They're one and the same."

Tears slipped down her cheeks. "Do you think that… we could skip out early on the rehearsal dinner? I think… I think there's a place I'd like to take you."

"Anything for you." We touched foreheads. "Except for a bikini wax. Saw that on the menu on the way in, never had clammier hands in all my life."

She laughed and wrapped her arms around me. "I love you."

My entire world shifted in those words as I let them surround me and hold me tight, and then I said them back. "I love you too."

CHAPTER EIGHTEEN

Phillipa

"Miraculous recovery my ass," Fitz muttered under his breath as the queen made her way into the room. The rehearsal had gone on without a hitch. We told the priest to hurry through it, mainly because we already knew what we were doing. We'd both attended more weddings than most people did in a lifetime.

And there was only one way a royal wedding was done.

Which made it terribly boring and easy.

I elbowed him and smirked. "She was sick, truly sick and in bed. Have a little heart for your soon-to-be mother-in-law."

"No. I don't buy it. Look at the way she's eyeing me, like she knows things, like she was sick on purpose, or planning something, or—"

"Actually sick." I patted his cheek. "You ready to go? It's a short walk from here."

"Ready when you are." Fitz handed his champagne to a passing waiter and offered his apologies to his mother, who didn't seem bothered in the least that he was leaving with me during dinner. It was casual since it was close family and a few friends. No fancy dresses, just a lot of alcohol, appetizers, and enough food displayed buffet-style to feed a small country.

It was what we'd wanted.

And in the end, everyone, including the queen, had agreed it would be best to have something casual since the wedding would be anything but.

I grabbed my coat, and then I grabbed Fitz's hand. Funny how I had lived so many years without his hand, and now I couldn't bear to walk anywhere without knowing he was right by my side.

He peered around me once we descended the steps into the bitter cold. "Good, you aren't bringing a shovel. I'm going to assume you aren't getting ready to murder me in the woods."

"Ha ha." I rolled my eyes as we took the worn rock path into the nearest tree line, and into a small meadow.

We walked a few more feet until I saw the marker. Even in the snow, it stood tall and proud, a white grave made for a king.

"I understand why my mother gave you the letters with caution. She knows how much I missed him. She knows how much it kills me to know that, even then, he was thinking about my future, about marriage. I just wish…" I felt the sting of tears. "I wish he was here to walk me down the aisle. I wish he was here so I could tease him and get teased in return while he shouts about being right."

Fitz pulled me against him and held on tight. "He'll always be here, Phillipa, just not in the way we selfishly want him."

I nodded and drew him with me toward the grave. Once we reached the bottom of the hill, I swiped the snow from his name and stood. "I miss you, Daddy," I said through tears. "And I wish you were here to walk me down the aisle tomorrow, but I think you'll be excited to know you were right, as always. It's Fitz, Daddy. He's… everything."

Fitz pulled me in for a hug and kissed the top of my head.

"I know if you were here, you'd be cleaning a gun or lecturing him on something, and as silly as it is, I still wanted you to have that chance." I touched the gravestone again as my hot tears fell and melted splotches into the snow.

"I know exactly what you would say, Your Majesty." Fitz's voice was solid, strong. It had always captivated me and did so even more now because he was addressing my father, his dead king, with respect even though he was in the ground. "You would laugh in my face, possibly tell me I needed to get a haircut, and then you'd ask me if I wanted to play chess." He grinned at me. "He always beat me, you know… I always said I let him, but we all knew the truth."

"I like that memory."

"Your Majesty…" Fitz locked eyes with me even though I knew he was still addressing my father. "There is one thing I need to do that I didn't get a chance to do." He put his arm across his chest and bent his knee to the ground. "I know I'm not worthy, but I'll fight every damn day to be better. I know there are thousands of other men, better men, but for some reason she chose me. I will lay my life down for Queen and Country, but most of all, I will take my queen's heart and love it the only way I know how, with everything I have in me. Your Majesty, may I please have the honor of marrying your daughter tomorrow?"

I couldn't see the grave in front of me from all the tears filling my eyes, but I didn't need to. It was a holy moment between two men, one still in this world, one in the next.

And I knew my father would be so proud.

I lifted my face to the sky and smiled just as the first snowflake fell, and when I opened my eyes…

It was snowing.

And I knew… it was a "yes."

CHAPTER NINETEEN

Fitz

It was a moment I'd never forget, an honor I wasn't worthy of, and a moment in time that would stay with me for as long as I lived.

I didn't sleep well that night.

Probably because Phillipa wasn't beside me.

That and the fact that my life was changing for the better, and I couldn't wait to marry her.

My queen.

I smiled throughout the morning as I slowly got ready. My staff and mother bombarded me for three solid hours.

I thanked God when Melly stopped by the room to slip something into my hand.

Whiskey.

The note attached said, "If I need this, you need ten."

God, I loved her.

I smiled and dumped it into my coffee then took a sip.

"Fitz!" Mother screeched my name, causing me to spill half my coffee onto the desk right on top of the manila folder containing all my soon-to-be father-in-law's letters.

"What?" I set the coffee down in a panic and pulled the letters out one by one, laying them flat so they could dry. The damage was minimal, but I nearly had a heart attack in the process.

"You look—" She covered her face with her hands and started crying. "You look just like your father."

This was the point where I should wince and take the praise. My father, in his last years, was bald and had a nose that looked more like Rudolph's than a human male's. I loved him desperately, but she was not exactly giving me a huge compliment, though I would claim his outgoing personality any day.

"I love you, Mother." I hugged her close.

She dabbed at her eyes and pulled away. "The cars are here. Have you decided who's to walk Phillipa down the aisle? The queen? You?"

I let out a sigh and looked over at the pages her father had written… then stared.

An idea hit so swiftly I felt like an idiot for not thinking of it before. "Her father."

"Excuse me?" Mother looked at me like I'd gone insane.

I grinned harder. "Her father will be walking her down the aisle." I handed her the papers. "Careful with the wet ones, and we'll need Melly's help with this."

THE ORGAN PLAYED the bridal march.

The doors were still closed, and I'd yet to see her.

In total panic, I wondered if she would even show up.

And then my paranoia worsened when I thought of her "father" walking her to the front of the church. Would she be too emotional? Would she care? Would she even like the idea?

The doors opened.

Everyone stood.

And all my fears faded away.

Phillipa beamed at me through her thin veil, clutching a picture of her father tight to her chest, the letters he'd written tied with a blue Christmas bow.

Something borrowed: The letters.

Something blue: The bow.

Something old: Her father's picture.

Something new: A daughter holding her father's picture as she walks down the aisle.

After all, traditions aren't always what they're cracked up to be.

The sleeves of her dress fell off her shoulders, showing creamy skin. Her makeup was understated to the point of looking so natural anyone would realize she didn't need any at all.

She was perfect.

Mine.

I could barely get my vows out without crying. My chest was tight, and I just wanted to kiss her.

When it was her turn to read hers, she was already crying. "Fitz, the first time I met you, I tried to kill you, it's true." The church laughed quietly. "You were always so annoying, mainly because you always challenged me, and I was so used to winning… until you. Every year I planned on ways to thwart you, and every year we battled. Until you went to university and I grew up. Until this mutual hate turned into something completely opposite, love and respect. My father clearly saw the sparks we were too stupid to see, but now that I look back, I realize they were there all along. I used to lament over not having many close friends, and then I realized with awful clarity that you were always there for me. When I scraped my knee, when I got my first car, when I had wine for the first time and you tried to convince me to have more. You were there, through the good, through the bad… So it only makes sense that you would be here now, ready to help me lead this country as my husband, and as my king."

My eyes welled with tears.

"I cannot wait to marry you, to have a future with you, and I can only hope we can be as wise as my father once was when we have children of our own."

"I love you," she mouthed.

I leaned in to kiss her.

And was thwarted by the priest, who cleared his throat. "By the power vested in me, I now pronounce you man and wife. *Now,* you may kiss the—"

I kissed her so hard I think the priest was singed from the heat. I pulled her into my arms, held her close, and clung to her like a lifeline.

We both broke away panting.

The queen chose that moment to stand and walk toward us.

The coronation ceremony wasn't to take place until the following year, so I wasn't sure if she was going to make a speech or tell me this was all a bloody joke.

"Ladies and gentlemen." The queen held her arms wide. "As you all know, the soon-to-be queen and king have been stepping up while I was ailing. I must confess I was merely taking a break and testing them to see if my suspicions were correct, and I'm happy to announce they were."

"Told you so," I said under my breath, earning an elbow from Phillipa.

She held out her hand, and the priest handed her the royal scepter. Stunned, I watched as the ancient red pillows were placed in front of the podium.

"Kneel," the queen demanded.

I helped Phillipa down and then joined her, facing the queen and the rest of the guests.

She touched Phillipa's right shoulder, her left, and finally her head. I shook as she did the same to me—I knew how heavy the scepter was. I also knew that it would be just like the queen to slip and hit me in the head. Furthermore, I was suddenly very aware that I was being made king.

"Rise." She stood back and bowed as she handed Phillipa the scepter. "To Queen Phillipa Marjory Answorth Belleville and King Fitzgerald Geraldo Belleville, long live the queen!"

"Long live the queen, indeed," I said loudly, drawing Phillipa into my arms and kissing her while the people shouted and cheered.

I didn't care.

Not about the titles.

Or the crowd.

I finally had her.

I didn't even register that a crown was being placed on my head until I felt its weight in the next minute; it was heavy, just like the diamond-encrusted one she was wearing.

But we knew how to share the load.
That was all that mattered.

CHAPTER TWENTY

Phillipa

I WAS MARRIED.

To a man I used to hate.

To someone I couldn't stop kissing.

I grinned at him as he made eye contact with me across the room. Everyone was dancing, drinking, and feasting.

And I was at the Christmas Eve Ball. Only this time, it was to celebrate my own wedding.

To the very person I remembered hating so much when I wasn't allowed to go in and celebrate.

"Look at us now," Fitz said once he reached me. "Did you ever in your wildest dreams imagine a day where we'd have a cease fire, wedding, and both be dancing at the ball without intentionally spilling punch on each other?"

"No, not at all, though I did get cake in your ear."

"Ah yes, and up my nose, and somehow in my eyes. Let's

just pray I don't go blind because you had to get too aggressive with the frosting."

"It's tradition." I laughed.

He just shook his head. "What am I going to do with you?"

"Lots of things..." I wrapped my arms around him. "In fact, I think we should go start them right now."

"Yep, brilliant idea." He grabbed my hand and weaved us through the crowd fast enough that people couldn't stop us and offer their congratulations.

We were spending Christmas at the castle and taking our honeymoon a week after New Year's.

And we'd decided to keep our rooms as they were.

Because something about waking up in his arms the way I did that first time felt right. I still had my room, but I was going to be sharing his until we left.

The way it should be.

I laughed as he stumbled trying to get the door open, and stopped laughing altogether when he slammed the door shut behind him, locked it, and immediately started kissing me senseless.

"God save me from so many damn buttons," he said, reaching behind me and trying to undo each one by one. "How many are there?" He fumbled with the third one.

"Here." I turned around while he quickly moved down my back and tried not to get too nervous about what I was wearing underneath.

The last button was loose. I stepped out of the dress, turned, and faced him.

His grin couldn't have been bigger if he tried. He wiped his hands down his face. "Please tell me this is every fantasy come to life for you too."

"Um, maybe not every fantasy." I shrugged. "But I figured it had special meaning."

"You..." He bit down on his lower lip and shook his head. "You're in a candy cane bodice with red panties. Please tell me you hid props."

I burst out laughing. "Sorry to disappoint."

"Hmmm, I may be able to rectify that." He pulled a small box out of his pocket and opened it facing me. "Great minds think alike."

It was a small silver candy cane charm on a beautiful chain. And on the candy cane was the date we were married.

My eyes filled with tears. "This is us."

"Even if it means only you and I get it, yes, our story is summed up with this one candy cane, and I wanted to make sure you always had a reminder of our love."

I nodded as I took it out of the box and fastened it around my neck. "You just may get lucky tonight."

"Yes, well, just in case you were too tired, I did record two of your favorites: one about a prince, the other about a waitress."

My eyes widened. "You really do love me if you forgo sex for Christmas movies."

His eyes penetrated, they drank me in, they held me. "Everything I do... is for you."

Movies forgotten, I pulled him into my arms and kissed him, long and slow, as he braced my hips with his hands and then very slowly drew the red lace panties down my thighs. "I think you should keep the candy cane bodice on. It's too sweet to take off." He gave a sly chuckle. "See what I did there?"

"Really? You joke now?" I huffed, kissing him again.

And then I was airborne as he held me in his arms. I

wrapped my legs around him, irritated that he had so many clothes on.

He stumbled back against the bed. We broke apart briefly as I tugged his shirt open, revealing hard muscle I wanted to rake my nails down. My heart beat harder the more I felt beneath my palms. He was so perfect, so mine.

He kicked his shoes off, and then his trousers went flying, followed by everything that divided us.

Skin on skin, everything was searing hot, perfect, like a fairy tale. I smiled against his mouth as he teased my entrance. "And they lived happily ever after?"

"Very." He moved against me. "Happily." I bit back a moan as he filled me completely. "Happily." Every movement was pure pleasure. "Ever." I shrieked as he rocked his hips. "After."

"Do that again," I demanded, raking my nails down his chest.

"Of course, Your Majesty… you just tell me how hard."

We laughed together, and I knew I would never look at a candy cane the same way again.

"I love you," I said against his neck as he took me higher and higher into oblivion; I saw stars, heaven. "So much."

"I love you too."

We let go, both of us together; it was a beautiful thing.

And when our sweaty bodies were still recovering, my husband reached over, grabbed the remote control, and flipped on a Christmas movie, whispering against my lips, "Anything for you, my treasure."

WANT MORE RVD?

Try these other RVD New Adult Romances!

CAPTURE

Losing your ability to speak at the age of seventeen; it's not normal or fair.

But trauma, has a way of throwing normality out the window.

Dani lives anything but a normal life.

Her sister is married to one of the biggest names in Hollywood.

Her best friends are rockstar duo AD2.

And she has more love around her than most people experience in a lifetime.

But that doesn't change the fact their parents are dead.

Or that it's her fault.

It seems her new normal is being a mute, living on the inside, unable to actually communicate on the outside.

That is until Hollywood's newest heartthrob Lincoln Greene hires her as his assistant for the summer.

He's gorgeous, completely unavailable, and unobtainable.

But that doesn't stop her from wondering… if things were different… would he want her?

If she was whole, would he be the other half?

KEEP

My name is shouted on rooftops.

It's written on bras, on the inside of bathroom stalls, hell my name is everywhere.

To say my name is to experience an orgasm without ever leaving your damn house.

My name is Zane "Saint" Andrews.

I'm sex.

I'm a rock god.

I'm also… a virgin.

What they don't know won't kill them right? Give the people what they want. And what they want is the idea of me; the pleasure they gain at listening to my song and knowing without a doubt I'm talking about them and only them.

It worked for a while.

Until a nerdy girl with glasses falls at my feet, literally, and suddenly I don't want to be Saint anymore, what I want? What I really need?

Is to be kept.

By her.

STEAL

It's easy to lose yourself in someone you love.

Easier to lose yourself in someone you hate…

I didn't think it could get any worse than having to babysit a bunch of spoiled musicians on set — keeping them out of trouble is a cakewalk compared to seeing my ex every day.

Seaside, Oregon isn't big enough for the both of us.

She hates me.

I loathe her.

The plan was simple — stay the hell away and make sure she gets to set on time.

What I didn't expect was to be faced with our past in front of an audience — and be forced to face it again.

It's torture.

The way she looks at me.

The way I try to look through her.

Words left unsaid.

The lingering aftermath still as powerful as ever.

I feed the chasm between us, for fear that she'll make me feel again — and steal the last shred of heart I have left.

We have everything but each other.

It's not enough.

Not when you've lost love.

And replaced it with the only thing left — hate.

RISKY PLAY

Even one-night stands deserve a second chance in *New York Times* bestselling author Rachel Van Dyken's novel of sporting desire.

What else can a virgin do when she's ditched at the altar? Seattle heiress Mackenzie Dupont is treating herself to a single-girl honeymoon in Mexico and a desire to relinquish her innocence to a gorgeous one-night stand. Fake names. True pleasure. But when she wakes up alone, Mackenzie realizes just how much anger is left in her broken heart.

Suffering a tragic personal loss, pro soccer player Slade Rodriguez has his reasons for vanishing without a goodbye. Right or wrong, he's blaming the beautiful and infuriating stranger he never wants to see again. They're both in for a shock when Mackenzie shows up as his new personal assistant. And they both have a lot to learn about each other. Because they share more than they could possibly know, including a common enemy who's playing his own games. And he's not afraid to get dirty.

Now there's only one way Mackenzie and Slade can win: to trust in each other and to stop hiding from the lies they've told, the secrets they've kept, the mistakes they've made, and the attraction that still burns between them.

ABOUT THE AUTHOR

Rachel Van Dyken is a *New York Times*, *Wall Street Journal*, and *USA Today* bestselling author. When she's not writing about hot hunks for her Regency romance or New Adult fiction books, Rachel is dreaming up *new* hunks. (The more hunks, the merrier!) While Rachel writes a lot, she also makes sure she enjoys the finer things in life — like *The Bachelor* and strong coffee.

Rachel lives in Idaho with her husband, son, and two boxers. Fans can follow her writing journey at www.RachelVanDykenAuthor.com and www.facebook.com/rachelvandyken.

ALSO BY RACHEL VAN DYKEN

Eagle Elite

Elite

Elect

Entice

Elicit

Bang Bang

Enchant

Enforce

Ember

Elude

Empire

Enrage

Eulogy

Envy

Elite Bratva Brotherhood

Debase

The Bet Series

The Bet

The Wager

The Dare

Seaside Series

Tear

Pull

Shatter

Forever

Fall

Strung

Eternal

Seaside Pictures

Capture

Keep

Steal

All Stars Fall

Abandon

Ruin Series

Ruin

Toxic

Fearless

Shame

The Dark Ones Series

The Dark Ones
Untouchable Darkness
Dark Surrender
Darkest Temptation

The Consequence Series

The Consequence of Loving Colton
The Consequence of Revenge
The Consequence of Seduction
The Consequence of Rejection

Wingmen Inc.

The Matchmaker's Playbook
The Matchmaker's Replacement

The Bachelors of Arizona

The Bachelor Auction
The Playboy Bachelor
The Bachelor Contract

Curious Liaisons

Cheater
Cheater's Regret

Players Game

Fraternize
Infraction
MVP

Liars, Inc

Dirty Exes

Dangerous Exes

Red Card

Risky Play

Kickin' It

Cruel Summer

Summer Heat

Summer Seduction

Summer Nights

Waltzing With The Wallflower

Waltzing with the Wallflower

Beguiling Bridget

Taming Wilde

London Fairy Tales

Upon a Midnight Dream

Whispered Music

The Wolf's Pursuit

When Ash Falls

Renwick House

The Ugly Duckling Debutante

The Seduction of Sebastian St. James

The Redemption of Lord Rawlings

An Unlikely Alliance

The Devil Duke Takes a Bride

Other Titles

The Parting Gift

Compromising Kessen

Savage Winter

Divine Uprising

Every Girl Does It

RIP

Co-Ed

RVD